GABRiEL FiNLEY
& THE LORD OF AIR AND DARKNESS

Also by George Hagen

Gabriel Finley & the Raven's Riddle

GABRiEL FiNLEY
& THE LORD OF AIR AND DARKNESS

GEORGE HAGEN

schwartz & wade books • new york

Text copyright © 2017 by George Hagen
Jacket art and interior illustrations copyright © 2017 by Petur Antonsson

All rights reserved. Published in the United States by Schwartz & Wade Books, an imprint of Random House Children's Books, a division of Penguin Random House LLC, New York.

Schwartz & Wade Books and the colophon are trademarks of Penguin Random House LLC.

Visit us on the Web! randomhousekids.com
Educators and librarians, for a variety of teaching tools, visit us at RHTeachersLibrarians.com

Library of Congress Cataloging-in-Publication Data is available upon request.
ISBN 978-0-399-55347-9 (hc)
ISBN 978-0-399-55348-6 (lib. bdg.)
ISBN 978-0-399-55349-3 (ebook)

The text of this book is set in 12-point Weiss.
Book design by Rachael Cole

Printed in the United States of America
2 4 6 8 10 9 7 5 3 1
First Edition

To Brooklyn,
beloved son, artist, and fellow fantasist

Prologue

Ravens love riddles—you may already know this if you have read the first Gabriel Finley adventure and want to jump ahead to the next chapter. But if you didn't know this, you may be surprised, perhaps even astonished, by what I am about to tell you.

Ravens, you see, greet each other with riddles, just as you might shake the hand of a stranger. One raven will bow to another and say something like this:

"What will make you smart with just a tap?"

And the other raven might reply, "A pin, because a pin-prick really smarts!"

Both will utter a raspy chuckle and they will become fast friends.

Long ago, these clever, mischievous birds were our most loyal companions. If a human answered a raven's riddle, he or she might become that raven's *amicus*—which means "friend," but something more as well. They could communicate without speaking, simply by telepathy, as well as *paravolate*, which means to merge together and fly, as one, above the trees and rooftops. Which of course was the most remarkable thing of all.

In those wondrous days, a raven watched out for you if you were his amicus. He warned you when a thunderstorm was coming, cheered you up when you were sad by telling jokes, and brought you medicine if you were sick or wounded in battle. Even better, if you were in trouble, your raven could rescue you, and take you aloft, far from harm.

Meeting a raven was thrilling, for if that raven asked *you* a riddle, it guaranteed many extraordinary adventures for the rest of your life.

But unfortunately, something very tragic changed all this.

During some foolish and misbegotten war, there was a battle between armies on a barren moor. Ironclad knights clashed for days while their foot soldiers fought with pikes and sticks. Nobody won, and those who survived fled, leaving the dead or badly injured behind. These wounded soldiers lay near death, attended only by their loyal ravens.

Just before dawn, a phantom bird flew down and alighted on a bare tree to survey the misery. At first glance, the bird resembled a raven because of its black satin feathers (although they were unusually tattered and thin). It had black talons (but they were jagged and gnarled from age). Its eyes were the most unsettling feature—they showed no joy, no kindness, no laughter, just a sickly, menacing yellow glow.

One raven, named Concord, was tending to a fallen

knight who was too sick to paravolate. All Concord could do was offer words of hope.

"Master, you must hold on to life," he whispered. "When the sun rises, its warmth will make you strong again!"

"Your human will not live to see the sun," interjected the phantom bird. "He will die, and then you will be friendless and lonely. But if you act now, you may gain something better than life itself."

Concord was puzzled. "What could that be?"

"Immortality!" replied the phantom. "Never to be sad or fearful of death again."

"Is it really possible?" Concord asked, for he saw death's hand all over the battlefield.

"Yes, you can cheat death. It's quite easy."

The phantom directed Concord to take one bite of his master's flesh. "After all," the creature said, "he's going to die anyway."

Trembling, Concord took a small peck from his master's wound. As he swallowed it, the last glimmer of life left his master's eyes and Concord realized he had done a terrible thing. But it was too late. His amicus had died, and some new transformation was happening.

The raven's heart beat faster and faster until the beats became one big roar. And then, inexplicably, it stopped. Just like that. No beat, no pulse—and yet Concord knew he was not dead.

An icy chill crept into his veins. He felt strangely

untethered and weightless and noticed a gap in his chest where his heart had been. The sun, a faint orange glow on the horizon, seemed to shoot across the sky as if time itself had released him from all restraints.

What has happened to me? he wondered.

"You are free—the minutes, hours, days have lost their grip on you," said the phantom bird. "You are immortal!"

In the weeks that followed, Concord watched the phantom recruit more ravens from the battlefields. The odd gap in his chest began to ache terribly. He realized he had made a devil's bargain—in exchange for immortality he felt an endless hunger, a joyless spirit, and great loneliness. All living creatures seemed to fear him because of an eerie yellow glow in his eyes.

When the humans began to notice these valravens—for that is what Concord and others who had eaten their masters' flesh were called—and the corpses of their amici, they became superstitious and fearful of any black bird. Waving swords and sticks, they drove all ravens away. Soon no raven dared approach a human lest he be attacked or caged. The phantom bird had divided ravens from their most trusted friends.

That would have been the end of my story, but for this:
Once in a while, a raven still *did* pose a riddle to a child.

Perhaps, just as we humans wish for good times, ravens do too. In these rare cases, a raven might strike up a friendship that lasts a lifetime. The first Gabriel Finley book described exactly that: the extraordinary adventures of one boy and a raven.

But what if a raven chooses the worst possible child?

A generation before Gabriel was born, there was another boy, named Corax Finley.

Corax was mean, with a smirk on his lips and dark, unruly hair that swept across his forehead. He was cruel to cats and dogs, and not much nicer to people. He lived in a neighborhood of Brooklyn on a tree-lined block full of tall brownstone houses with flickering gaslights.

Corax was walking home from school one day when a voice in his head interrupted his thoughts.

I have no will, no heart, no soul.
I'm flat and smooth and stiff in back.
All who see me stop and stare,
And if they smile, I'll smile right back.
What am I?

Corax didn't know any riddles. In fact, he hated riddles. They were annoying and stupid and a waste of time. He was about to ignore the voice when he noticed a raven watching him. Perched on a fence, it had a deep, intelligent stare. It bowed to him and seemed to be waiting eagerly for his answer.

Corax struggled to think of one. Finally, he said, "Is it a clown?"

The bird shook its head.

Wrong. Try again tomorrow!

The bird flew away. Fascinated, Corax stared after it. How had its voice entered his thoughts? And what would happen if he answered its riddle correctly? He decided to be ready for its return.

Corax knew a girl who was quite good at riddles. She was a friend of his sister; he had always ignored her, but now he realized she might be useful to him.

"My friend Trudy likes you," his sister Jasmine once told him. "She would do anything for you."

When he found the girls at home that afternoon, Corax softened his voice and looked into Trudy's bright sapphire eyes.

"Hey there," he said. "I have a riddle for you . . . ," and he repeated the words he'd heard.

Trudy seemed delighted to have Corax's attention.

"Hmm . . . no will, no heart, no soul," she replied. "It sounds like something that's not alive. Flat and smooth and stiff, something that people stop and stare at, like a picture, or a TV screen, or a . . ." She suddenly became excited. "Wait! People stop and stare at a mirror! And *if* they smile, the reflection smiles back. Could it be a mirror?"

"Very good!" said Corax, as if he'd known the answer all along, and he bounded upstairs.

"I have a feeling he just used you to find out the answer," Jasmine said.

"Oh, I don't mind," Trudy replied.

Even the cruelest or most careless people can have a strange power over others. This was true of Corax. Trudy would have answered many more riddles for him.

After school the next day Corax found the raven at the very same spot.

"I have the answer," he said. "It's a mirror."

The raven bowed. *Correct,* he said, again without speaking. *My name is Silverwing. Will you be my amicus?*

"What's that?" asked Corax.

The loyal friend of a raven. It is an ancient tradition. A raven and his amicus may talk telepathically, and paravolate, *or fly as one,* the raven explained.

So I can just think *what I want to say to you and you'll hear it— like this?* asked Corax in his head.

Exactly.

But Corax was even more excited about the possibility of flying. *Show me how we paravolate,* he said.

Pay attention, said Silverwing. *Raise your arms and take enormous breaths until every particle in your body seems to tingle. Then jump!*

Corax did as he was instructed. For a brief instant he was

terrified. He felt crushed and cramped as he merged with the raven's muscles and bones, and heard the deafening beat of Silverwing's heart (much faster than any human heartbeat). Then this cramped feeling passed and Corax saw that he had a new body—satin wings, a handsome black beak, and slender talons.

Now that the two souls were one, they took off, soaring above the fences, the oak trees, the rooftops, and chimneys until they were circling the borough of Brooklyn with its perfectly arrayed streets and chockablock houses. They swooped over the glittering East River, the Brooklyn Bridge, the ships moored in the bay, the blinking lights of the Verrazano Bridge and the Coney Island Wonder Wheel.

By the time Corax got home that evening he was giddy thinking about all the things—out of reach to normal people—that now lay within his grasp.

The very next afternoon, he and Silverwing landed on the sill of an open window of a tall building. They entered, and after poking around, stole a ring with a bright sapphire stone.

Once Corax started stealing, he couldn't stop. They entered open windows all over the city and took anything that shone, sparkled, or gleamed.

Corax gathered the spoils from these flights on the shelves of his bedroom. He had jars of medals, jars of gold rings, jars of garnets, amethysts, and rubies, necklaces and bracelets.

There were boxes of earrings, velvet bags of coins and wrist-watches. He had so much fun stealing that he stayed out later and later each evening.

One night, after Silverwing had returned Corax to his bedroom and the boy sprang back into his own body, he noticed a silhouette standing in the doorway.

"So," said Dr. Ulysses Finley. "You answered a raven's riddle?"

Corax was startled by his father's question. "How did you know?"

"You are not the only one in this family who has been a raven's amicus," the doctor answered.

At that moment, a large raven landed on Dr. Finley's shoulder. Flexing its wings, it directed a stern gaze toward the jars on Corax's shelves.

"When I was your age I answered a raven's riddle, too," said Dr. Finley. "This is Humboldt." Both the raven and Dr. Finley frowned at Corax. "But you, my boy, are the first to use your new powers to steal. I'm deeply disappointed, and I forbid you to use this gift for such mischief."

After school the next day, Corax found that his father had removed all the jars and boxes. Immediately, he threw open his window, summoned Silverwing, and took off over the rooftops.

*   *   *

In the days that followed, Corax swooped down and stole from fruit stalls, newsstands, and candy stores. He flew over people, using his human voice to scare them. Each day his mischief grew worse until, one evening, he taunted a boy so badly that the terrified child ran into the path of a passing bus.

Realizing, for once, that he had done something terrible, Corax hurried home. He separated from Silverwing, entered by the front door, and went upstairs to his room.

There he found his father driving nails into his window frame.

"What's going on?" Corax asked.

"You will never fly again," his father said.

"But I didn't do anything!"

Dr. Finley gazed with disappointment at his son. "Humboldt has just informed me that a boy has been killed because of your cruelty. I should take you to the police, but I'd have to explain that my son had merged with a raven. . . ." Corax's father winced. "Instead I must punish you myself. Humboldt will take Silverwing away tomorrow."

"No!" cried Corax. "He can't!"

His father regarded him sadly. "He can and he will."

That night, Corax moaned and wailed in his bed. His cries were pitiful at first, then furious, then frightening. Finally, there was quiet, and the Finleys believed the worst was over.

But a crash of shattering glass and splintered wood woke

the family. Corax's parents hurried upstairs to find the room empty. The boy and the bird were gone.

Dr. Finley turned sadly to his wife. "I believe Corax has fled with his amicus. We may never see him again."

Although Dr. Finley's prediction was correct, Jasmine did glimpse her brother at unexpected moments over the years—in a crowd or watching her walk with friends down the street. Over time, it became obvious that he only appeared when she was with Trudy. She guessed that he had not forgotten that Trudy helped him solve that riddle, and might help him again.

Ten years later, another Finley child answered the riddle of a raven. The child was Adam, Corax and Jasmine's little brother. From his raven, Baldasarre, he found out exactly what had happened to Corax.

He killed his companion, Silverwing, the bird explained. *Then he ate the bird's flesh and was transformed into a hideous creature, half human, half raven. Now your brother rules over all valravens and countless other birds, in a domain called Aviopolis—a city built of marble and gemstone inside a vast underground cavern. It was constructed a thousand years ago by an army of warrior dwarfs. A towering citadel stands in its center, and Corax commands his valravens from its battlements.*

"Where is this place?" asked Adam.

Deep below us, but I warn you . . . Corax has his eye on the world above. He seeks to rule it.

"How could one person do that?" asked Adam doubtfully.

Ravens and valravens have fought for centuries over a magic necklace called a torc—a silver semicircle with a raven's head carved on both ends. Forged with black magic, it grants the wearer any wish. But every wish is bestowed with a horribly malicious twist, and most come to regret their wishes. It is pure evil. Corax sent his valravens across the world to find it.

"I don't understand why anyone would want it," Adam replied.

For its power, said Baldasarre. *If you thrive on tragedy and misfortune, the torc will serve you well. But no decent person would want it. Ravens have tried to keep it far from reach. In Corax's clutches, it would be like putting a spark to a keg of gunpowder; the torc will seek to flourish, and imperil a million souls.*

"Then my brother must never find it," Adam decided.

In time, Adam went to college and studied myths of all kinds. He found evidence of the torc in several ancient manuscripts that confirmed its amazing power.

Adam's university sent him to Iceland to continue his studies. He met his wife, Tabitha, there. Shortly after their son, Gabriel, was born, he learned of the tomb of a king buried with a mysterious wishing necklace.

Could this be the wicked torc, forged in black magic? Adam wondered.

He hiked into the northern caverns to find the tomb, but fell into a crevasse and gashed his leg. Limping and weary, he stumbled on until he arrived at a chamber filled with an ancient king's possessions. A warning was written on the walls:

Forged a thousand years ago, conceived with wicked glee,
Be wary, stranger, of the curse this torc bestows on thee.
Take heed, take care, and look out! We caution every host,
For it will boldly steal from you what you may cherish most!

But there was no necklace to be found, so Adam took the plainest-looking stick from the chamber to help him hobble back.

As he made his slow return through the caves, his flashlight battery died, and he became lost in the darkness. "I wish I could get home," Adam whispered to himself.

Suddenly, his leg stopped hurting, his flashlight lit up, and the difficult hike became much easier.

That plain, ordinary stick, you see, had the notorious torc wrapped around one end, concealed by centuries of dust and grime. The torc had granted Adam's wish . . . with one dreadful catch.

For when Adam arrived home, his baby, Gabriel, was in his crib and a hot meal waited on the table—but his wife, Tabitha, was nowhere to be seen. She had vanished the moment he walked through the door.

The words on the tomb wall had warned him to no avail:
For it will boldly steal from you what you may cherish most!

Brokenhearted, Adam gave the evil torc to his amicus,
Baldasarre, and asked him to hide it, then went back to his
old home in Brooklyn with his baby son.

When Corax was advised by a valraven that his brother
had found the torc, he returned to the Finley house to claim it.

Adam had been an infant when Corax fled as a boy, so
when the two men faced each other, they were startled to
see the same dark eyes and curly hair in the other. The resemblance was so striking that it might have brought them to
smile and embrace if Corax had not suddenly thrust out his
hand. "Give me the torc," he demanded.

"What? I don't even know where it is," Adam explained.
"My raven, Baldasarre, has hidden it so skillfully that only
my son—your nephew—Gabriel, will be able to find it. If
you try to harm him before that time, the torc will be lost
forever."

Corax was furious. "Then you'll be my hostage until the
boy is old enough to come looking for you!"

And so he took his brother to Aviopolis, in effect leaving
Gabriel an orphan, to be raised by his aunt Jasmine.

The hero of our first story (and of this one, too), Gabriel
Finley, had a passion for riddles. When he turned twelve, he
answered the riddle of a raven named Paladin, became his

amicus, and went on a dangerous but successful quest for the torc, just as his father had predicted.

With the torc and its staff in hand, Gabriel, Paladin, and several of Gabriel's best friends ventured to Aviopolis to bargain for his father's release. In a dangerous duel of riddles, Gabriel defeated Corax, but Corax seized the torc and made one devastating wish: for the torc's enormous power to enter him.

The wish backfired. Uttering agonized cries, Corax's soul was ripped from his body, which vanished in a flash. His formless presence hovered, bewildered and enraged, over the scene of his defeat.

From overhead, Corax's lieutenant, a robin named Snitcher, fluttered down and seized the necklace. With the torc wrapped around his neck, the dim-witted bird fled the collapsing city of Aviopolis.

Gabriel and Paladin pursued the robin, but they lost track of him. Dodging the shattering rocks and tumbling rubble, they emerged into the cool night air of Brooklyn just as the entrance caved in on itself.

It appeared that Aviopolis was sealed for good and their troubles were over. Gabriel had rescued his father and they had safely escaped with Gabriel's friends. But his victory over Corax was tainted by one regret: he had lost the torc.

Up above the twinkling lights of Brooklyn, the gleeful robin savored his stolen prize—until his happy mood was interrupted by a voice in his head.

Ah, my little lieutenant, it is good that we are together.

"Who spoke?" sputtered the robin.

It is me, Corax, your lord and master. It appears that the necklace you're wearing contains my soul.

"What?" said the worried bird. "Where is the rest of you?"

I wish I knew, but you shall remain my servant until the day I find it.

❋Tabitha Finley❋

The weeks after Gabriel had rescued his father were the happiest the boy could remember. It was January, and his father took him for bike rides, to movies, and for pizza at their favorite restaurants in Brooklyn. They strolled along the waterfront as barges and ferries passed by, and went sledding down the snowy hillsides of Prospect Park.

During these moments they tried to catch up on the years they had been apart. Mr. Finley wanted to know about the friends—Pamela, Abby, and Somes—who had helped Gabriel rescue him from Aviopolis; he asked who Gabriel's best and worst teachers were and tried to answer his trickiest riddles. He wanted to hear about Gabriel's hobbies and his favorite books, and where the tastiest dumplings could be found in the neighborhood.

Eventually, they got around to discussing a more serious matter—the torc—and how it had caused Gabriel's mother to disappear when he was just a baby. On a sunny day father and son went kite-flying in the park. Mr. Finley released a seven-foot multicolored kite into the sky, and as it soared and swooped above them, Gabriel asked his father a question.

"Dad? Could you please explain exactly *how* Mom disappeared?"

Mr. Finley lowered the kite string and looked at his son with gentle surprise. "Yes, of course," he said. "I've been waiting for you to be old enough to understand. You had just been born, and your mother and I were living in a little turf-roofed cottage in Iceland," he began. "One day I went hiking in the caverns where there was a tomb—"

"Oh, I know that part," Gabriel interrupted. "And I know how you got injured, and made a wish to get home, and your leg healed and you realized that the torc was on the staff you were using to help you walk. And when you did get home and stepped through the front door, you saw me, but—"

"Your mother vanished into thin air," said Adam.

He paused to play out string and watch the kite float higher above the river.

"The torc answered my wish, but its price was to ruin me. One minute Tabitha was there, as full of life as anyone can be—and the next she was gone."

Now Gabriel had to ask the dreadful question that haunted his dreams and lingered on the edges of his wakeful thoughts.

"Dad, is she dead?"

Adam accidentally jerked on the kite string. "Dead? Oh, my goodness. Absolutely not! If she were, I would feel it!"

"How?"

For a moment, Adam Finley looked embarrassed. He was a professor, a logical man who cited evidence to prove his points. He hated to admit that a feeling could be more significant than a fact. He chewed at his beard for a moment. "Well, I can't explain it."

Then he frowned at the kite and began to turn the string winder to draw it nearer. "I believe that when the torc makes people disappear, it splits them—soul from body. I think Tabitha is alive because . . . well, because I *sense* her with me."

The professor looked worried that his son might laugh, but Gabriel seemed relieved.

"Dad, has she ever talked to you?"

"No. I just feel her presence." Mr. Finley looked anxiously at Gabriel. "Has she talked to you?"

"No, but . . ." Gabriel shrugged. "Sometimes I feel the same thing. She's here, somewhere." He raised his hand to his heart and rested it there.

"Ah." Adam nodded. "So it's a matter of figuring out how, um . . ."

"To bring her back?" offered Gabriel.

Before Adam could reply, a gust almost wrenched the metal string winder from his grip. "Good heavens, this wind is quite strong," he said. "Help me."

They both wrestled to hold on to the winder, but *snap!* The frayed end of the string whipped away, and the untethered kite flew upward until it was lost in the great blue sky.

The two of them stared bleakly into an infinity of blueness.

"Oh well," sighed Adam at last. "It's just a kite."

As they walked back along the path, Adam continued their conversation. "Gabriel . . . I am quite determined to find your mother. I promise you that. We will bring her back."

"How?"

"Well, the one thing we know about the physical world is that nothing just disappears. That kite, for example, will land somewhere."

"We just don't know where," said Gabriel sadly.

"Don't lose hope," said Adam. "On Monday I go back to teaching my classes, but I'll use every spare minute I have to find out where 'disappeared' things go."

"What can I do?" asked Gabriel.

"Continue with school, of course," replied his father. "Teachers, classes, homework, the usual."

Gabriel's heart sank. How could he possibly go back to the usual when his father had raised the possibility of bringing his mother home? School was so boring after rescuing his father from a prison cell and defeating his demon uncle in a duel of riddles, not to mention escaping a collapsing underground city.

"But I want to help find Mom," he said. "Don't forget, I have my own amicus, Paladin. We could paravolate all over the city and even farther."

"And there are plenty of valravens loyal to Corax who would relish capturing you, especially for revenge."

"But I've fought valravens before. Paladin and I fought an eagle! And we have birds on our side, like the great horned owls!"

"Gabriel?" Mr. Finley suddenly became stern. "I don't want you to paravolate."

The boy's shoulders dropped. "But why? I'm not like Corax when he was a kid."

Adam laughed. "I wasn't suggesting you are."

By now, they were walking beneath the span of the Brooklyn Bridge. The slick gray current of the East River rolled by with immense power and speed.

"Dad?" said Gabriel, finally. "Do you remember me telling you about the robin named Snitcher who stole the torc after Corax vanished?"

"Yes, you followed him out of Aviopolis and he disappeared."

"Well, what happens if he makes wishes with the torc?"

"Very good question," replied Mr. Finley. "Have you seen him?"

"No, but if I do, shouldn't I try to get the torc back?"

The professor paused for a moment to think. "I'm not too concerned about a robin," he said at last. "They have such small brains; they're much more likely to take orders than give them."

"Whew," said Gabriel. "I was worried about that."

❋ Snitcher ❋

And what *had* happened to the robin?

In the weeks since the fall of Aviopolis, Corax's little red-breasted lieutenant had been enjoying his freedom in the blue skies of Brooklyn. He didn't miss digging for ugly gray grubs or sipping from the murky puddles of Corax's gloomy underground domain. Now he enjoyed pink worms, dough-nut crumbs, and pizza crusts.

In fact, the robin regretted stealing the torc because it weighed so heavily around his neck. He had tried to shake it off, but it grew tighter when he resisted it. Snitcher might have tolerated this, too, but for the voice that spoke from the necklace.

Snitcher? Where are we? said the voice one frosty morning as the robin settled upon a smoking chimney to warm himself.

The startled robin glanced around. "Who said that?"

It is I, Corax, you fool. . . . Have you forgotten that my soul is trapped inside this thing?

Indeed, with each word, the torc shook with fearsome intensity. The robin gulped.

"Dear master," he replied, "we're in a place called Brooklyn. Your great citadel is rubble and dust."

Then my valravens must be awaiting my orders. I have a domain to rebuild. We must find my body! I must plot my revenge!

"How would I know where your body is? You're just a voice in my ear," replied the robin.

This reply infuriated Corax. *How can I rule like this? Formless, adrift, lost . . . I must wish myself free!*

The puzzled robin waited expectantly.

Several moments passed without any bright flash, tingle, or transformation.

"Master?" said the bird finally. "What's taking so long?"

It seems I am helpless, replied Corax. *This torc binds me as tight as manacles and leg irons.*

The voice stopped, as if thinking.

Snitcher, I have an idea, it began again. *Perhaps if you were to wish me to be united with my body, it would obey.*

"Yes, Your Eminence!" The robin puffed out his scarlet chest, and his two beady black eyes trembled as he tried to concentrate (a staggeringly difficult task for a robin). "I wish that my master, Corax, the Lord of Air and Darkness, were whole and standing here before me."

Again, nothing happened. The torc hung around the robin's neck like a dull trinket.

"Hmm," said the robin. "Perhaps it is broken, Your Eminence."

Broken? Corax's voice turned scornful. *Impossible! It answered* the Finley boy's wishes. He brought down my citadel and destroyed Aviopolis.

"I think it's broken," repeated the dim bird.

Black magic does not break, muttered Corax. And if my soul is trapped in this torc, what has become of the rest of me? Where does the body go when the soul is cast adrift?

"It's all Gabriel Finley's fault. He brought down your citadel and destroyed Aviopo—"

I just said that! snapped Corax.

"The Finley boy should be destroyed," suggested the robin. "That would solve all your troubles. Useless child. And his father. I bet he broke the torc."

Silence!

They were a most unhappy pair. The robin wouldn't stop talking and Corax wouldn't stop telling him to be quiet.

Eventually, however, something uttered by Snitcher gave Corax an idea. "I've watched them through the window," the robin confessed. "The boy shares riddles with his raven, the father reads from his wall of books—"

That's it! Adam Finley has studied the torc for years. The boy and his father understand its power. They must hold the key to my freedom.

"I know the way to their house," said the robin.

Very good, Snitcher. We must listen at their windows. Go there now!

"Yes, Eminence." Snitcher took to the air and flapped over the rooftops of Brooklyn while the cumbersome torc bore down on his neck.

Presently, he began to feel tired and hungry. "Your Eminence," he pleaded, "I'm starving. Surely first I could—"

I command you to go to the Finley house!

In moments, the frightened robin had flown to a window on the topmost floor of an old brownstone on Fifth Street. He perched on the windowsill, then peered into the room, with its single occupant.

It was a boy around twelve years old, asleep in bed. Upon a bed knob was a very handsome raven with black satin feathers and a ruff of single quills around his neck. This was Paladin.

The raven had been sleeping with his head tucked under his wing, but grew alert when he heard a sound. His neck feathers rose in alarm, and he turned to the window.

The robin stared back at him, his little black eyes ruthless and vengeful.

Gabriel, wake up! There's a robin at the window. I'm positive that it's Snitcher, with that wicked torc around his neck.

Paladin's silent message woke Gabriel, who quickly rubbed the sleep from his eyes and sat up. He squinted at the window and saw the little bird through the pane of glass. Then he noticed the indentation around the robin's scarlet breast.

"You're right, Paladin," he replied. "But my dad said there's no safer place for the torc than around a robin's neck—they're followers, not leaders."

Paladin scrutinized the robin. *I'm not so sure your father is correct. I don't like the look in that bird's eyes.*

As Gabriel got dressed, Paladin raised his wings and flew at the window, issuing a threatening cry. The startled robin staggered backward, and toppled out of view.

From downstairs, a voice announced breakfast. Gabriel set Paladin upon his shoulder and hurried to the kitchen.

Adam Finley was eating breakfast beside a tall, spindly woman with red hair bound in a topknot. This was Gabriel's Aunt Jaz, Adam's sister. She was a schoolteacher. Her faint eyebrows were drawn in with dark mascara to resemble two little boomerangs, which gave her an expression of perpetual surprise.

"Good morning, Gabriel," she said. *"Bonjour,* Paladin."

"Bonjour, Madame," said Paladin, bowing to Aunt Jaz.

Gabriel glanced curiously at Paladin. "I didn't know you spoke French."

"I'm teaching him a little each day," explained Aunt Jaz. "He's a quick learner."

At that moment, a girl about Gabriel's age entered the kitchen. "Good morning, Mr. Finley, Aunt Jaz," she said.

"Oh, good morning, Pamela," said Aunt Jaz.

Pamela had a sensitive, yearning expression, deep brown eyes, and long, curly dark hair. She and her mother had been living with the Finleys since their apartment building had burned down last year. Pamela set her violin case by a chair and went to the stove to prepare some oatmeal.

Mr. Finley glanced up from his newspaper to see Pamela pour water into a saucepan and set it on the burner. "You know," he whispered, "the stove could make that for you."

"What?" asked Pamela.

At that moment, Pamela's mother, Trudy Baskin, entered, and Adam slyly put a finger to his lips, hinting that this was not a subject to be discussed in front of her.

Although Trudy had once loved riddles, and solved one as a favor for Corax long ago, the years had changed her. She had cropped gray hair and piercing blue eyes, and a pinched, irritable personality. Gabriel didn't know much about her past, but he felt pretty sure that some unpleasant event had erased her sense of humor and fun.

This morning he braced himself for Trudy's first words.

"Oh," she said, noticing Paladin on his shoulder. "You brought that filthy bird downstairs."

"He's not filthy," Gabriel replied.

"He's full of germs."

"We're *all* full of germs," countered Gabriel. "That's a fact."

"It's a filthy fact." Trudy sniffed.

Gabriel uttered a soft sigh, which earned him a sympathetic smile from Pamela. She understood his special relationship with Paladin. As one of the three friends who had helped Gabriel rescue his father from Aviopolis, Pamela knew all about paravolating and valravens and the power of the torc.

Pamela most envied Gabriel because of the Finley family

history of bonding with ravens. She wished she could be a raven's amicus and fly, as he could.

"Well, I must be off," said Aunt Jaz, finishing her coffee. "I have a new teacher to welcome at school today. Gabriel, are you coming?"

Gabriel had just plucked his toast from the toaster, so he waved to Aunt Jaz and explained that he would walk with his friends.

"Okay. Have a nice day, everybody!" said Aunt Jaz.

As the front door slammed, Pamela gave a wistful sigh. "I wish my school were just down the hill instead of a long subway ride away."

"My dear child," said Trudy. "Your school is superior to Gabriel's school. You have a scholarship, music lessons, and a fine future ahead of you."

Gabriel tried to defend himself. "There's nothing wrong with my—"

"Oh, look at the time!" interrupted Mr. Finley. "I should be off. By the way, you should all go ahead and have dinner without me tonight. In all likelihood, my research will keep me late."

"Really, Dad?" Gabriel exclaimed. "Are you going to find out where 'disappeared' things go?"

"Disappeared things? What on earth are you talking about?" said Trudy suspiciously.

"Like . . . socks," said Gabriel hurriedly. "Dad's socks disappeared and he needs to find them."

His father smiled and headed upstairs to the front door.

"Oh, look! There's a robin at the window," said Pamela.

The scarlet-breasted bird was jumping up and down with great excitement on the other side of the window. However, the moment Gabriel turned to see it, the bird fluttered away.

"Oh, what a pretty little fellow!" said Trudy. "I love robins. They're such sweet birds."

"Actually, they're not sweet at all," Gabriel said. "And they're stupid."

"What an ignorant thing to say about such an innocent creature," said Trudy. "You couldn't possibly know anything about robins!"

"It just so happens I know . . ." But with one look at Trudy, Gabriel realized it was hopeless to argue. "Oh, never mind!"

Outside the Finley house, the exuberant robin had landed on the high branch of a magnolia tree. He couldn't contain his excitement, flapping his wings and chirping.

"Did you hear what he said, Eminence? Where *disappeared* things go!"

Indeed, replied Corax. *I'll wager that Adam Finley is looking for a lost soul of his own—I believe the boy's mother vanished by the torc's magic, too. I shall profit from his endeavor. Quick, we must follow him.*

"But I'm hungry!" the bird whined. "I must eat first."

Control yourself, Snitcher! scolded Corax.

"Oh dear, if I don't eat I might faint," muttered the robin to himself. "I *wish* I had something to eat right now."

At that moment, the torc began to glow a pale blue upon the robin's scarlet breast, and its sudden warmth startled him. "Ooh!" cried Snitcher. "Something is happening!"

What did you just do? cried Corax.

"Nothing. I just . . . *wished*, and now the torc is burning hot!"

Then it isn't broken, declared Corax with a note of triumph.

"What's it going to do?" chirruped the robin.

The answer to that question didn't come immediately, although both Corax and the robin sensed that something momentous was about to happen. Would the torc simply grant the robin's wish, or would it respond in some strange, catastrophic way?

❈ The Blizzard ❈

Gabriel stepped outside and slung his backpack over his shoulder. The air felt oddly charged, like the moment before a thunderstorm when the sky darkens and the wind picks up. A thick cluster of clouds had swept over the bright azure sky, and a fierce gust whipped leaves and twigs into swirling eddies along the sidewalk.

"Something's weird around here," said a voice that made Gabriel spin around.

"Oh, hi, Abby," he said.

Abigail Chastain's frizzy blond hair was arranged into twelve short pigtails across her scalp, and she wore cat's-eye glasses and mismatched clogs (one red, one green). She had been a vital member of Gabriel's group during the rescue of his father and was, like Gabriel, a riddle fanatic. Abby had no mild opinions—she either loved or hated things. Some people found her annoying for this reason, but Gabriel considered her a great friend, especially in times of danger.

"There's something in the air. Do you feel it, too?" asked Gabriel.

"I feel magic," said Abby with a giddy smile. "Hey, look up there!"

Gabriel looked skyward. A cluster of clouds seemed to turn in a slow circle—like cream in some vast overhead mixing bowl.

"Magic," said Abby. "It's the only explanation. Let's see if Somes agrees."

Somes Grindle was the fourth member of their group. His house was a gray clapboard building just two blocks away. Gabriel and Abby walked with breathless steps up to the front door and knocked. A shingle that read GRINDLE swung wildly in the wind as a tall man stepped out, wearing a white baker's uniform and carrying a lunch box. He looked at the kids and yelled roughly inside, "Somes, your friends are here!"

"Good morning, Mr. Grindle," said Gabriel.

Mr. Grindle answered with only a sigh. Then he winced and rubbed his hand.

"Did you hurt yourself?" asked Abby.

"It's that blasted pain in my hand," he muttered. "I've had it for years, but it's bad this morning for some reason. Must be the weather." He looked up at the spiraling thunderclouds. "Somes is late, as usual. Maybe you two can get him to school on time." With that, Mr. Grindle nodded goodbye and hurried down the street.

Now a tall boy with a thick thatch of brown hair and black-framed glasses emerged from the house. Somes looked like his father, but he was lankier. His worn jeans were loose on his frame, he wore no socks, and each canvas sneaker was held together with a single frayed shoelace. After locking the door, he kicked a battered backpack down the stoop, then lazily threw it over his shoulder. Somes hated homework, and this was his way of showing it.

"What's up?" said Somes. Like Abby and Pamela, he had been with Gabriel on the journey to Aviopolis to rescue Gabriel's father.

"We think there's something in the air," said Abby.

Somes sniffed suspiciously. "Yeah, something. That smell. It's not electric, but—" He interrupted himself to point upward. "I've never seen clouds do *that*."

The clouds were slate gray and churning in a swift spiral directly overhead.

The three friends began walking hurriedly downhill toward school.

"It smells like magic!" Abby's eyes lit up as she turned to Gabriel. "I told you."

An explanation popped into Gabriel's mind. The clues were obvious—strange atmospheric activity, magic, and the appearance of the robin on his windowsill. "It must be something to do with the torc." Gabriel told them about the robin he had spotted earlier that morning.

"Why didn't you try to catch it?" asked Somes.

"Yeah, why?" said Abby.

Now Gabriel felt annoyed with himself. "Well, because

my dad said the torc couldn't do much harm around a stupid bird's neck."

The three friends were on the last block before school. The clouds directly above were whirling in a furious gray froth.

"That robin might wish for anything," said Somes.

"Actually, I think it would probably only wish for a few things, like food, or—ooh!" Abby looked up with surprise. Little white flakes were falling through the air. She held out her hand. "Snow!" she said.

"But it's not cold," said Gabriel.

"And it's not snow," said Somes. "It's—"

"Birdseed!" said Abby. She had licked a few of the particles that had landed on her hand.

"Canary seeds? Sesame seeds?" said Somes.

"Sunflower seeds, too," murmured Gabriel.

By this time, they had arrived at the steps of the Alfred Grimes Academy, a stately old building with scrolled sandstone carvings above the windows and doors. The most prominent was of the head and shoulders of an elderly man with a patch over one eye. He peered down with a wry smile at the students. This, apparently, was Alfred Grimes, and his sardonic countenance might have had something to do with the school's motto: *Vita Mysterium*, or Life Is a Mystery.

Several teachers raised their collars and waved students hurriedly inside as particles whipped and spun in the air around them. Nobody else seemed to notice that the flakes weren't snow. Aunt Jaz stood beside an unfamiliar figure, a man in his fifties with receding hair and a dark beard.

"New teacher," Gabriel said to his friends. "Aunt Jaz told me."

Suddenly, Aunt Jaz uttered a high, tumbling laugh.

"Seems like your aunt likes him," observed Somes.

The wind was blowing wildly now, and the particles were everywhere—in students' hair and all over the sidewalk.

"Children! Come in, come in!" instructed Aunt Jaz.

Reluctantly, the three merged with the crowd entering the building, their shoes crunching on freshly fallen canary seed.

Meanwhile, a group of frenzied pigeons swooped down to investigate this blessing from the skies.

The math teacher was late, so Gabriel laid his books on his desk and peered through the classroom windows at the street below. The clouds had pulled away like a curtain to reveal a perfect blue sky. There was no indication of the bizarre weather except for hundreds of birds darting about, pecking up seeds from the gutters and pavements.

"Definitely magic," whispered Abby.

"Positively," added Somes, joining them by the window.

"The robin made a wish," Gabriel said. "That's the only explanation."

Abby's forehead creased with worry. "But if he can wish for something like this, maybe he's not so harmless."

At that moment, the teacher entered. It was the man they had seen talking to Aunt Jaz. He wrote his name on the board.

There was a collective gasp as the students read the name: Mr. Coffin.

"That's right," the teacher said. "My name is Coffin, and I'll be your substitute for a few months until Mr. Delgado recovers from his juggling injuries."

Abby's hand shot up. "Was it knives again?"

"No," replied Mr. Coffin. "Live animals . . . porcupines, I believe."

After a buzz of chatter, Mr. Coffin called for silence and rolled up his sleeves.

This drew more surprised gasps, because his forearms were covered with tattoos. But instead of words or pictures, they were mathematical formulas.

"These are my favorite equations," he said. "And they come from Newton, Euclid, and Descartes. You might say that those men are my heroes. Because of them, we can calculate a planet's orbit, or the path of a rocket, or the surface of a sphere. Perhaps they'll become your heroes, too."

Somes groaned and slumped down, resting his chin on his desk.

Mr. Coffin noticed his reaction. "You, sir, what's your name?"

"Somes Grindle."

"Mr. Grindle? Can you tell me how to define a circle?"

"It's, um . . ." Somes looked helpless for a moment, but then he seemed to surprise himself with an answer. "A shape where all the points are the same distance from the center."

"Very good. Indeed, it's a bit like your group of friends," said Mr. Coffin, his eyes darting from Gabriel to Abby to Somes. "Yes, all the same distance apart, held together by something. What? *Magic*, perhaps?"

This remark startled all three of them.

"Magic. What did he mean by that?" said Gabriel later.

They were in the cafeteria at lunch, huddled together, talking in low voices.

"Maybe he noticed the birdseed," said Abby.

"Or he knows something about us," Gabriel suggested.

"That's the first time I ever answered a class question correctly," Somes told them. "There's definitely magic in the air."

"Well, I think he's interesting," said Abby. "You can't go around with a name like Coffin without being a little mysterious."

"You just love a mystery," said Somes.

"Nothing wrong with that," Abby replied.

Not far from school, a robin alighted on the gutter of a tall house and began gorging on the sunflower and canary seeds that lay at his feet. His little black eyes were bright with triumph.

"I'll never be hungry again! I can wish for whatever I want!"

Snitcher, I hope you haven't forgotten me, said a menacing voice.

The robin felt an unpleasant tightness around his neck. He wriggled slightly, but the necklace grew taut until he could barely breathe.

"Eminence," he gasped, "I could never forget you. I was just so hungry!"

Do not disobey me again, or you will be sure to regret it, Corax replied.

The necklace squeezed again, and the suffocating robin uttered a frantic chirp. "But I only wanted a bite of—"

We have lost a chance to follow Adam. I want you to return to the Finleys' windowsill and stay there.

"Yes, Eminence," the robin croaked.

As the necklace loosened around his throat, the relieved robin obediently spread his wings and took flight.

❀ The Magic Stove ❀

"**O**h, gosh!"

Pamela was very disappointed to have missed the bird-seed blizzard. She had returned from school to find the others talking about it in Gabriel's kitchen.

"Well, it proves one thing," said Somes.

"What's that?" asked Gabriel.

"You can be dumb and still be dangerous. What if that robin wished to be ten stories tall and went on a rampage across the city, crushing buildings under its feet like King Kong or something?"

"It only wished for birdseed," said Abby. "That's pretty logical for a bird."

"Yeah, but remember those robins in Aviopolis?" said Pamela. "Corax made them his jailers; they controlled all the locks and cages. They liked being more powerful than the other birds. Snitcher perched on Corax's shoulder and repeated his commands."

"For sure," said Gabriel. "Snitcher is no ordinary robin."

"So why do you think he's hanging around your house?" asked Somes.

Nobody had an answer for this.

Abby stroked Paladin, who was perched on Gabriel's shoulder. "Any ideas, you beautiful bird?"

The raven bowed to her, dipping his beak low and extending one foot, but he did not speak.

Abby frowned. "Gabriel, why won't Paladin talk to me?"

"He's just shy," Gabriel explained.

"He speaks French to your aunt," Pamela reminded Gabriel. "But she's kind of a weird bird herself."

Abby turned to the raven. "But you *know* me, Paladin."

He nuzzled her cheek with his beak to show that he didn't mean to offend her. Abby gave a sigh. "It's my birthday in a week, and the only thing I really, really, *really* want is—"

"I know," Pamela said.

"Me too," added Somes. "You want to be a raven's amicus."

"Exactly!" Abby cried. "I want a raven friend like Paladin, a friend who understands my deepest thoughts. And I want to fly."

"Yeah. Flying," agreed Somes. "Every time my dad loses his temper, I could just step outside with my raven and take off."

"Tell the story again, Gabriel. How did you find Paladin?" asked Pamela.

"I heard his thoughts in my head," Gabriel explained.

"Just talking. I couldn't see him. For a while, I knew someone or something was near. And then the night that his mother was killed by valravens, I found him on my windowsill, shaking, and that's when he asked me a riddle."

Abby turned bleakly to Paladin. "How can I find a raven, Paladin?"

The raven stared off for a moment, then turned to Gabriel.

"He said it's like making friends," explained Gabriel. "You can't predict when you'll meet one; it just happens. My dad said it runs in our family."

Abby looked downcast. "In other words, there's no chance it'll happen to me."

"No chance for me, either," said Somes glumly.

"Or me," said Pamela. "Hey, speaking of your dad, Gabriel, he started to tell me something weird this morning. . . ."

"What?"

"He said your stove would cook me oatmeal if I asked it. Then my mom came in, and he stopped talking."

Gabriel turned to the antique iron stove. It was an odd contraption with curved legs, a broad black surface, and six circular lids. The front had cream-colored hatches, dials, and a row of four black holes above them. "Weird," he said. "My aunt never told me it could cook by itself. Sometimes it does make strange knocking noises, and she tells it to be quiet. I always thought she was just kidding around."

"What if we could get it to cook for us?" said Abby.

Gabriel peered at the griddle, squeezed the knobs, and twisted the bar that opened the oven hatch. "Hello," he said.

The contraption remained silent.

"I like custard," said Somes. "Hey, Stove, make custard!"

"Yeah, can you make custard, Stovie?" said Abby.

Gabriel raised one of the griddle hatches and talked into it. "Hi in there? Make custard!"

Pamela, who had been watching her friends' efforts with impatience, finally shook her head. "You're doing it all wrong."

"Really?" Somes replied. "How many stoves have you talked to?"

"For your information, I've talked to a writing desk."

Only Somes laughed when she said this. That was because Abby and Gabriel knew that what Pamela said was quite true. The Finley house contained at least one other odd piece of furniture. It was a black writing desk with front legs carved like the talons of a bird. When no one was looking, the desk moved from room to room, evading discovery. The word ASK was inscribed on its polished lid, and if you asked it a question, it might reveal a remarkable answer. Mr. Finley used the desk to hide valuable information, but it was a very elusive, disagreeable piece of furniture, and Gabriel and Abby had once risked great injury trying to get it to reveal its contents.

Quite by accident, Pamela had discovered that the desk was fond of music. She was practicing her violin one evening, and it scurried up the stairs to her room and began dancing on its taloned feet. It was particularly fond of jigs and other Irish tunes.

Pamela explained all this to Somes, but he remained skeptical.

"Can we try talking to it respectfully?" she asked.

"You mean like calling it Mr. Stove?" said Somes.

"Maybe it's a Mrs.," added Gabriel.

"Or a Ms.," said Abby.

"You're being silly," Pamela replied. She kneeled before the stove, pulled the oven hatch open, and spoke in a whisper. "Hello. Please, would you be willing to make us some custard? We would all really appreciate it."

There was a loud clatter. A metal arm holding a wire whisk emerged from one of the recessed holes; it stretched, as if stiff from years of inactivity. Then it knocked sharply on the other holes, as if to wake them up.

A second arm with pinchers extended toward the pantry cupboard. A third one reached across the room for a mixing bowl. In a flash, the arms began pouring salt and sugar. The whisking arm cracked the eggs and whisked them into a froth with dizzying speed. A small pot heated the milk in seconds, and the mixture was ready in another blink. One arm presented a mug of warm custard to Pamela.

She took a sip and uttered a gasp. "Oh, wow!" she said. "That's so good!"

Another mechanical arm swiftly delivered mugs to Gabriel, Abby, and Somes.

"Yum!" said Somes. "I'm eating here tonight."

"I wish my sister could make this," said Abby. "She's a good cook, but this is *awesome*."

Suddenly, a voice called down the staircase. "I smell custard!"

The arms from the stove shot back into their holes, leaving the whisk flipping through the air. It landed in Pamela's open hand.

Trudy entered the kitchen. She dipped her finger in the custard pot, licked it, then frowned.

"Wonderful, quite wonderful."

To everyone's surprise, a sweet, regretful look appeared on her face. "I used to make desserts, long ago," she said. "Pastries, cakes, custard, and chocolate. Chocolate cookies, chocolate cakes and candies." She sighed. "Not many people know that chocolate is very bitter to the tongue. It's unpleasant until you mix it with sugar and a pinch of salt. . . . You might say that chocolate is like love that way."

This odd remark surprised them all, but none more than Pamela. "Mom?" she said. "What are you talking about?"

"Love can be a bitter thing," Trudy continued. "It breaks hearts all the time. Think of all the sad songs there are about love. Love is only sweet when it's combined with other things—trust, affection, compassion, and forgiveness."

Gabriel had never heard Trudy say anything so thoughtful or tender. He wondered if she was sick.

"Tell me, who cooked this heavenly custard?" she asked.

Gabriel decided to tell her the truth. "Actually," he said, "the stove made it."

Trudy's eyes sharpened into needles. "Pardon me? What on earth are you talking about?"

Gabriel shrank back as she glared at him.

Abby rushed to defend him. "Mrs. Baskin, Gabriel was about to explain that this stove is very good for making custard, and Pamela got it to work for us."

"Pamela? Oh, you mean *she* cooked it? Well, of course, I'm not surprised." Trudy sniffed. "Another fine cook in the family!"

She took one more sip of custard. "It's time for me to make dinner, so I'd appreciate it if you would all vacate the premises."

Gabriel took Paladin upon his shoulder. He was about to lead his friends to his room when Somes pointed to the window. "Look!"

They all turned and saw the silhouette of a robin on the windowsill.

Quickly, they scrambled after it into the backyard.

❖ The Worm ❖

Confronted by four children and a raven, any normal robin would quickly flutter away, but Snitcher was not normal. As he perched on the windowsill, his nasty little black eyes scrutinized the four friends one by one. He seemed to recognize Gabriel, and threw out his chest boldly. Around his throat, the torc began to glow with a pale blue light.

Paladin uttered a loud *CAW!* and flew at the robin, but Snitcher eluded him in a zigzag flight over the fence before vanishing into a thick holly bush next door. The children watched the raven circle the bush until the robin flew out and, in a matter of a few seconds, both birds disappeared over a rooftop.

"I hope Paladin catches him," said Gabriel.

"Did anyone notice the torc?" said Somes. "It glowed."

"Yeah," said Abby with concern. "And does anyone feel what I'm feeling?" She looked down at her feet.

A deep rumble filled their ears, and they felt their feet trembling as if they were standing on a subway platform.

Gabriel noticed that the soil was also shaking; every particle seemed to be alive.

"Guys!" he cried. "Get back in the—"

Before he finished his sentence, the ground beneath him gave way and he dropped into a dark cavity. It was warm, slimy, and pitch-black, and it closed so tightly around Gabriel that his shout of panic collapsed in a stifled gurgle. He felt wet and enclosed from every side. *This is what being swallowed alive feels like*, he thought as he struggled. His arms were glued to his sides, and though he could still kick his legs, he felt quite sure that he had only a few breaths left before smothering to death in utter darkness.

"Hey, where did he go?" screamed Abby.

The answer to her question arrived abruptly as a large, segmented pink creature burst out of the hole. Abby thought it was pink toothpaste at first (if there could be a tube as wide and long as a subway car). It kept coming out of the hole, then curled along the fence in the yard, then doubled over itself several times in loops and swirls.

"Oh, my God," gasped Pamela.

The creature had no limbs and no eyes, just a long, fleshy, pink body glistening with slime and dirt. It squeezed its way out of the hole, undulating and pulsing, and finally settled in a vast, overlapping heap.

"Gabriel!" cried Somes. "Where are you?"

"I know what this is," said Pamela with disgust. "It's a humongous worm."

"*Lumbricus terrestris* is a worm's scientific name," Abby explained, "but this one should have a new name: *Lumbricus terrestris giganticus!*"

"I'll bet you the robin wished for it," said Somes. "Doesn't it make sense that a robin would wish for a worm?"

"Good point," said Abby. "Maybe it was only the length of my finger a few minutes ago."

Abby, Somes, and Pamela ventured nearer the creature. It groaned and twitched in the chill air of the evening, apparently overburdened by its own vast weight.

Somes noticed that one end had a wrinkled hole at the tip. "Gabriel?" he cried. "Can you hear me?"

A muffled cry answered.

"Oh, Gabriel!" cried Pamela. "Are you okay?"

A bulge near the end trembled slightly, a hint that Gabriel was inside, and alive.

"He got swallowed." Somes aimed a kick at the worm's midsection, which it absorbed without any kind of reaction. He threw all his weight at the creature. This time, the head reared up at him with a hiss.

"Somes, careful!" cried Abby.

The boy sprang backward as the worm's head rose above him, then dropped, striking the ground with such force that the three children bounced off the pulverized earth.

Somes retaliated with a fresh kick. The worm shifted with a languid twist, which emboldened Somes to creep nearer.

"Don't, Somes!" cried Pamela.

"Gabriel's inside," Abby reminded him, furiously rubbing her eyeglasses. "A worm has no teeth, but we've got to get him out before he gets digested by its stomach acids."

Pamela cupped her hands and shouted, "Gabriel, we'll save you!"

A weak grunt emerged from inside the worm.

"I hope he's not getting dissolved yet," said Somes.

Abby crept closer to examine the bulge near the worm's puckered mouth. "He must be right here."

"Maybe we can force its mouth open," said Pamela. She had noticed the handle of a shovel lying beneath the worm's coils. Dragging the shovel free, she raised it over her head and tried to poke the worm's mouth. It opened and, with a sucking noise, swallowed the shovel whole.

Pamela blinked. "Big appetite."

"I'd probably stay away from that end," reasoned Somes.

Abby pressed her fingers to her temples, trying to think. "Let's see . . . a worm's body is mostly stomach. It's going to squeeze Gabriel farther down its intestine until he's dissolved. I know! We need to make it vomit!"

"Isn't there something you can get at a drugstore that makes you throw up?" replied Pamela.

"*Ipecac*," said Somes. "But we'd need fifty buckets of it."

"Hey, did you see that?" Pamela pointed at the worm's undulating segments, which were squeezing in ripples along the length of its trunk.

The bulge—which they guessed was Gabriel—had just moved farther down the worm's body.

"Oh, this is a nightmare," said Abby.

This seemed to inspire Somes. He picked up the garden hose that lay in a coil by the wall of the house. Grabbing the nozzle, he turned to the others.

"I'm going to get under that thing and throw the hose to you from the other side."

"Wait. Why?" cried Pamela.

"Just think 'tube of toothpaste.'" And with that, Somes dove under the worm.

There was a tense moment as the girls waited.

"I made it!" came his muffled voice at last. "Here, catch this and slip it back under to me."

In a second, the hose nozzle flopped over the top of the worm's trunk and fell at Pamela's feet.

She grabbed it, kneeled, and wiggled the hose beneath the worm's body.

After a few more throws, the creature was encircled near its middle by several layers of garden hose. "Now pull!" yelled Somes from the other side of the worm. "Hard as you can!"

Leaning back, the girls pulled the hose taut with their combined weight.

On the other side of the worm's trunk, Somes knotted his end around one arm and pulled in the opposite direction.

After several pulls, the worm's midsection resembled the

narrowest part of a link of sausages. It must have been painful because the creature squirmed and uttered a horrific bellow. "*Oooiuuub!*"

"Again!" cried Somes, pulling with all his might.

Suddenly, the worm's head reared up and flailed left, then right, and with a wretched heave, the creature blew a pool of slime from its mouth. This was followed by the shovel, which clattered to the ground. Finally, a large object shot out and landed in a lump on the ground.

It did not move.

Abby flew beside it and began scooping away layers of glistening intestinal mucus until her friend was revealed. "Gabriel," she said, shaking him. "Are you okay? Are you? Are you?"

"Blech." Gabriel spat slime out of his mouth.

Abby slumped against him with relief. "He's okay!"

The enormous worm stirred now. Segment by segment, it slid backward, trying to retreat down its entry hole. This would have been good news, except for the fact that one end of the garden hose was wrapped tightly around its middle and the other end was knotted around Somes's arm. It pulled him across the patio.

"Somebody grab me!" he cried. He struggled to untie the knot, but he couldn't disentangle himself fast enough, and slid helplessly toward the hole.

"Oh, Somes!" cried Pamela, running over to anchor him.

Their combined weight was still no match for the enormous creature. Both Pamela and Somes were pulled toward
the hole.

Gabriel had just wiped the slime from his face when he
saw what was happening. "Where's the shovel?" he cried.
"We've got to cut the hose!"

Gabriel tried to get up, but he slipped on the pool of
slime beneath him.

Abby sprang for the shovel, seized its slimy handle, and
swung it down sideways at the hose. She missed, swung
again—and this time cut it cleanly. The severed hose followed the worm into the crumbling hole while Somes collapsed at its edge with Pamela clutching his feet.

As the group wiped handfuls of mucus from their clothes,
Somes turned to Gabriel. "First a birdseed storm, then a
worm that swallows people," he said. "What the heck made
your dad think that robin was harmless?"

Inside, Trudy had the radio on and was busily cutting up
vegetables at the kitchen counter. The group hurried past her
and ran up the stairs, two steps at a time. They were dazed,
but also giddy at having defeated the worm. In the upstairs
bathroom, they crowded around the medicine cabinet and
passed ointment and bandages to each other.

"Why is the robin watching you, Gabriel?" said Abby as

she placed a large bandage on his elbow. "I mean, there must be a reason."

Somes smeared ointment on his nose. "To get his revenge, of course," he replied. "Don't forget that when Gabriel defeated Corax, the robin lost everything. He stopped being important and went back to being a simple robin—"

"Are you kidding?" said Pamela, taking the ointment from Somes to dab her forehead with it. "Do you think a robin can remember all that, eavesdrop at Gabriel's window, *and* arrange a worm attack?"

"Do you have a better idea?" asked Somes.

Abby put a bandage on the bridge of her nose and replaced her glasses. "I think Pamela's right. This is too much for a robin's little brain. That bird is getting advice from someone," she declared.

Trudy made seaweed stew that evening. It was every bit as disgusting as it sounds. Three varieties of bulbous seaweed were mixed with rubbery noodles, then topped with small podlike things that resembled dead tadpoles. Normally, Gabriel would spread Trudy's concoctions around the edge of his plate and empty them into the trash later, but Trudy gave him a large helping and watched him take the first, second, and third bites.

After dinner, everybody gathered to wash and dry the

dishes. Aunt Jaz was about to pass the copper pot to Gabriel to dry when she noticed her reflection in it.

She paused, frowning. "Trudy, dear?" she said anxiously. "Do you think I should wear my hair down around my shoulders more often?"

Pamela's mother gave a skeptical sniff. "You've had it pinned up for years. Why change it now?"

Aunt Jaz sighed. "Oh, sometimes I wish I looked . . . younger."

Trudy regarded Aunt Jaz suspiciously. "Why? You're the same age as I am, Jasmine. There's nothing wrong with our age."

When Jasmine noticed that Gabriel and Pamela were staring at her, she lowered the pot and smiled faintly. "Don't mind me, dears. I'm just being vain."

Gabriel knew that his aunt was not the kind of person who admired herself very often in the mirror. "I think you look nice, Aunt Jaz," he said.

"Me too," added Pamela.

"Thank you, both of you," she replied. Aunt Jaz stole another glance at herself and her little black boomerang eyebrows rose wistfully. "Well, that's enough daydreaming. I've got a long night of homework to correct."

"And I'm taking a bath," said Trudy.

Gabriel looked at Pamela after they'd left. "What's going on with my aunt?"

"Maybe she's in love," said Pamela, smiling.

"Do old people fall in love?"

"Oh, Gabriel," said Pamela.

Gabriel looked at her. "Do you think your mom has ever been in love?"

Pamela shrugged. "She must have loved my dad, but she's never ever talked about him. He died when I was a baby."

And with that, she hurried up to the top floor, to her bedroom. Moments later, the sweet sound of her violin echoed through the house.

Gabriel padded up one flight to his father's study. He'd decided to do his homework there, where he enjoyed the odd smells of varnish, old leather, paper, ink, and cherry tobacco. He entered and curled up in a large leather armchair, hoping his father would get home soon with good news.

But the hours wore on. Gabriel finished his work, and began to doze off.

He was woken by tapping at the window. It was Paladin, who looked breathless and excited.

What a night! exclaimed the raven once Gabriel had let him inside. *Every time I thought I had caught that twit, he dodged away. I've never known a robin to be so clever. After a while I began to think that he was guided by somebody else.*

"Abby thought the same thing," remarked Gabriel, and he told Paladin about the worm's attack.

I should have been at your side, Paladin said. *What if I'd lost you?*

"It's really okay," Gabriel said, giving him a gentle stroke.

The two chatted for a few more minutes, and then Gabriel fell asleep in the armchair with the raven nestled in his lap.

When he awoke in the morning, Gabriel found himself back in his own room. Paladin was at his usual spot on the bed knob. Gabriel's father must have come home and taken him up to bed.

❊Elixirs and Secrets❊

That next morning, as the household ate breakfast, Gabriel tried to catch his father's eye. But Mr. Finley seemed to be deep in thought, staring at his coffee.

Eventually, Trudy left the house with Pamela, and Gabriel began to tell his father the details of his struggle with the giant worm.

"Good heavens!" said Mr. Finley. "I'm relieved that you and your friends were able to escape unharmed; you all showed extraordinary bravery."

"Not me," admitted Gabriel. "I just got swallowed."

"Ah, but you thought of using the shovel to free Somes. If friends stand up for each other, they can survive anything."

"Dad, we think the robin made a wish, and the torc delivered a giant worm."

"That's a good theory," said Mr. Finley.

"Abby and Paladin think Snitcher is getting advice. What if I paravolate with Paladin and get the torc back from him before something worse—"

"Paravolate?" interrupted Mr. Finley. "No, I forbid it, Gabriel. You've been in enough danger already."

Gabriel looked glumly into the milky remains of his cereal. But then he had a hopeful thought. "So what about yesterday? Did you find out anything about how to get Mom back?"

"All last night I pored over the only book I know on the subject of disappeared things, and it's all—"

"Yes?" said Gabriel anxiously.

Mr. Finley gave a weary sigh. "It's all written in Gutnish, a language I hardly understand. I could be studying another ten years before I find what I need to know."

"*Ten years* before you can bring Mom back?"

Mr. Finley put his hand softly on Gabriel's shoulder. "I won't give up, Gabriel. But it may take a long time."

Gabriel's heart sank. Just a few days before, the prospect of finding his mother seemed so close. He sat stirring the milk in his bowl, trying to rally his feelings into some hopeful thought, when his eyes strayed to the stove.

"Hey, Dad?" he said. "Pamela got the stove to cook custard for her yesterday."

"I'm not surprised," said Mr. Finley. "You know, it's a *mojo-mechanism*, just like the desk."

"A *mojo*-mechanism?"

"That's correct—a charmed object with an independent sense of purpose," said Mr. Finley. "Your aunt never liked using it; she felt it was cheating to cook with magic all the time. It happens to be very good at beef stroganoff and makes a dandy pineapple upside-down cake."

"Where did it come from?"

"Oh, I bought it years ago from that shady fellow, Pleshette, who has the shop on Union Street."

Gabriel remembered visiting Pleshette the year before. A snippy, disagreeable man, the shopkeeper grudgingly gave him advice on feeding Paladin—although he had been more interested in *buying* Paladin so that he could sell him for a lot of money.

"Pleshette runs a very disreputable business," said Mr. Finley. "The stove could make rash potions, which he sold for high prices."

"What are rash potions?"

"They're ill-considered or reckless medicines," said Mr. Finley. "He sold an elixir that would keep a child looking the same age forever. In one terrible case, a woman ran out of the potion and her five-year-old suddenly turned into a fifty-seven-year-old who still couldn't tie his shoelaces! It's a lesson for anyone seeking eternal youth."

"The thing I don't understand is why Pamela is so good with magical stuff," said Gabriel. "She got the stove to cook on the first try."

Mr. Finley's eyes narrowed slightly. "Well, these things run in families."

"But Trudy isn't . . . I mean, she doesn't even believe in magic. So it must have been Pamela's dad. Who was he, anyway?"

"Look at the time," replied Mr. Finley. "I've a class to teach." He jumped up with surprising vigor and disappeared up the stairs.

Gabriel stared after him, puzzled. Mr. Finley had many secrets. Every time he revealed one, he would expose another mystery that needed to be solved.

❊ What Runs in the Family? ❊

The weather for the rest of the week was normal. That is to say that no odd things fell out of the sky, and nothing gigantic came bursting out of the soil. Still, Gabriel's father had forbidden him to go into the backyard in case the worm or the robin returned.

Gabriel kept an eye out for Snitcher on his windowsill, but he didn't see him. Nevertheless, he had the uncomfortable feeling that he was being watched.

Each day, as he and his friends walked home from school, they kept a lookout for the robin. Abby was also on the alert for ravens because she remembered that Gabriel had answered a raven's riddle around the time of his twelfth birthday, and her birthday was in just a few days.

"I'm practicing riddles, just in case," she said.

By now it was the middle of February. One morning the icy puddles melted, the skies became clear, and the days grew pleasantly warm, at least at midday. It might have been a wintry lull (or the work of a wishful robin). Gabriel's friends chose to enjoy it by gathering on his stoop after school.

"Who wants to ask me a riddle?" said Abby.

"Okay," said Gabriel. "What's broken whenever it's spoken?"

Abby frowned. "Broken whenever it's spoken. Hmm. Most riddles depend on the double meaning of a word. What's another meaning for *break*? The dawn breaks when the sun rises. Waves break, but they're not *broken*. Ooh! I know!" She turned to Gabriel. "Is it silence, because if you say the word, you break the silence?"

"That's it!" said Gabriel.

Abby rubbed her glasses. "I'm trying to solve at least five riddles a day," she said. "It would be a catastrophe to cross paths with a raven and not be ready for it."

"Aren't you missing one important fact?" said Somes.

"What?" said Abby.

"Bonding with ravens runs in *Gabriel's* family. Your chances of meeting one are really slim."

"Somes, don't jinx me!" Abby cried. "What if I told *you* that the one thing you wanted more than anything else was totally impossible to get?"

Somes shrugged. "Sorry, but you're not a Finley."

Gabriel changed the topic. "Pamela, what do you know about your dad?"

"He left when I was a baby, and his name was Ramsey. Ramsey Baskin," she replied. "Why?"

"Oh, it's just that my dad wasn't surprised that you got

the oven to cook. When I asked why, he said magic runs in the family."

"You know, every time I ask about my dad, my mom changes the subject," Pamela said. "I don't even have a picture of him."

Abby turned to her with excitement. "Pamela," she said, "you've got to find out the truth. If your mom hasn't told you anything, there must be a reason. And what if it's a really incredible reason?"

The holly bush in the yard next to the Finley house had needle-sharp leaves that deterred cats as well as larger birds. It was the perfect hiding place, and Snitcher had been using it as his base since eluding Paladin.

His vicious little black eyes watched the children on the stoop. "Just one wish and I could turn the boys into grubs and the girls into—"

You'll make no wishes, commanded the voice in his head.

"But, Eminence, they are our enemies! If that worm had succeeded—"

You foolish, obstinate bird, I gave you no order to wish for a worm, snapped Corax. *How am I to accomplish my release if you disobey my commands?*

"Eminence, we do not need them," Snitcher persisted. "The older Finley is the only one who matters."

I have my reasons.

"I know what to wish," continued Snitcher. "I'll wish the brown-haired girl would turn into a delicious earwig—"

Of all those children, she is the one you must never harm! Do you hear me?

"But why?"

I am tired of your questions. Do my bidding and fly to the graveyard.

The robin was about to argue, but Corax's order was emphasized by a tightening sensation around his neck. Impelled by fear, he spread his wings and flew into the air.

Within moments, he had forgotten about Corax's puzzling command never to harm the girl with long brown hair.

It was dusk when the robin arrived at Cemetery Hill. He alighted in the crook of a tree, where he could not be seen. As the sunset faded from pale pink to a deep nocturnal violet, a wailing wind circled the mausoleums and obelisks, and several tatty black birds, their eyes glowing a sickly yellow, alighted on the headstones nearby.

"Greetings, Dreadbeak!"

"Good evening, Clutcher. Is there news?"

"We heard thunder beneath the ground earlier in the week. A monster worm lurks therein. Nobody knows how it came to be."

"Any word from our lord and master?"

"Alas, not yet," muttered Clutcher. "Perhaps Hookeye knows."

The valraven turned toward a particularly large and decrepit valraven with one yellow eye. His craggy beak was tipped white with age, his sparse feathers revealed yellowed bones and ribs, and he was perched upon the stone head of a winged baby, drumming his jagged talons upon the cherub's forehead.

"It has been months, brothers, since the disappearance of His Eminence," said Hookeye in a gravelly voice. "We remain determined to find him, and to renew our conquest of the sunlit world."

"But we have searched everywhere," replied Clutcher. "Aviopolis is a maze of ruins; it might take a hundred years to visit every chamber."

"I feel his presence in my bones, he is close, his spirit unites us," growled Hookeye.

"Piffle!" protested Dreadbeak. "Your bones are falling to bits. The spirit you feel is damp air blowing through dry flesh and tatty feathers. He's gone. He's kaput. He's—"

But Dreadbeak never finished his sentence. Hookeye flew at him with a merciless cry. *CAW! CAW!* Talons extended, the one-eyed phantom ripped at the other valraven, snapping at his throat and wings with his razor-sharp beak.

When Hookeye was done, Dreadbeak had been scattered in pieces upon the cemetery grass. But because he was immortal, his claws and wings squirmed by themselves, attempting to rejoin with his other parts.

"Let this be a lesson to every one of you!" said Hookeye, looking with disgust at the rest of his flock. "We may live forever, but I can still tear you apart, limb from limb. The next valraven that crosses me will spend the rest of eternity in search of his own head."

Snitcher watched in absolute horror, his scarlet breast heaving.

It is time for you to speak, robin, said Corax. *Tell them I am here. Inside you.*

"What?" Snitcher's little black eyes darted back and forth. "Must I? What if they don't believe me?"

Do as I say!

The robin fluttered anxiously from the tree and landed upon a tombstone to face the flock of valravens.

"Greetings, valravens!" he chirped. "It is I, Snitcher, lieutenant to the Lord of Air and Darkness, and I bring good news."

"Indeed, robin." Hookeye regarded him with a hungry sneer. "What say you?"

"His Eminence speaks to me through this torc I'm wearing. He is inside it, doomed by its mischievous curse to be separated from his body. He desires that you all follow my commands."

"But you're just a robin," muttered another valraven.

"I speak for His Eminence! He desires your help to reunite with his body."

"You don't *sound* like him," said another.

"If you disobey me," warned Snitcher, "you'll suffer the wrath of Corax!"

The shabby ghouls converged on the robin. "Prove it, boastful one!"

"What can I do to make them believe me?" mumbled Snitcher.

Make a wish, of course.

The robin's black eyes darted from one valraven to the next, relishing the chance to teach them a lesson. *I wish,* he thought, looking at the valravens. Suddenly, the torc glowed. There was a bright flash of blue light and three valravens flapped their wings in panic. Two of them froze in midair, then fell to the ground, shattering into stone fragments. The third remained attached to a headstone, solid as rock, as if carved by a stonemason.

A valraven hopped upon the headstone and tapped the unfortunate bird with his beak. "Still as stone," he murmured.

Hookeye turned to the robin. "If His Eminence *does* speak to you," he growled, "then tell me how old I am, for I am Corax's most loyal valraven. I found him in the frosty reaches of the north, after he left his family and ate the flesh of his own raven. He alone knows my age."

Four hundred and sixty-three.

The robin thrust out his chest and repeated, "Four hundred and sixty-three!"

The old valraven dipped his head, extending one foot in a stately bow. "Very well. Then a thousand valravens await his command."

❈ Who Was Ramsey Baskin? ❈

It was early Saturday morning when Pamela padded downstairs to find her mother sitting alone at the breakfast table. The house was quiet; everybody else was still asleep. All night, Pamela had been mulling over Abby's words. *You've got to find out the truth.* So she sat down at the table and fixed her eyes upon her mother with a steady and resolute gaze.

"Mom, I need to know about my dad."

Trudy Baskin didn't look up, but her chin began to tremble slightly. "What is it you want to know, dear?"

"Who was he and what happened to him?"

"Well, I've been expecting that question," admitted Trudy. "And I'd like to be able to tell you. But the truth is . . ."

Excited, Pamela leaned forward. "What?"

"The night you were born, I lost my memory. And your father disappeared."

"But you always told me he died."

"Died or vanished—I'm not sure which is worse," Trudy replied. "All I know is that something terrible happened that night. The last thing I remember was seeing a hideous raven with one yellow eye."

"No way," said Gabriel when Pamela shared her mother's explanation. "How could he just disappear? And why was a valraven the last thing she saw?"

It was later that Saturday afternoon, and the four were clustered on Gabriel's stoop. They were shivering because a cold snap had descended over Brooklyn. Pamela didn't want to talk inside, where her mother might overhear them.

"A sudden disappearance," said Somes. "Sounds like someone in *your* family, Gabriel."

"Yeah, but I know what my mom looks like," replied Gabriel. "I have pictures. How could Pamela's dad be a total mystery?"

"Doesn't your mom have wedding pictures?" asked Abby.

"Nope," Pamela replied. "And she said all his stuff vanished into thin air."

"No uncles, aunts? Other family?" added Gabriel.

"She doesn't remember."

Abby threw up her hands. "Totally impossible!"

"Do you think she was lying?" asked Gabriel.

Pamela shook her head. "I think she was very scared and she's afraid of remembering what happened."

"Hmm," said Somes. "So she remembered a raven with one yellow eye?"

"I guess that explains why she doesn't like ravens," said Gabriel.

Abby sprang up from the step, delighted. "This is too cool! You have a mysterious father who completely disappeared when you were born, and the only thing your mother remembers is a valraven."

"It doesn't feel cool," Pamela said wistfully. "I have a zillion questions and zero answers."

"Hey," said Gabriel, "maybe it's time to ask the writing desk."

Gabriel was, of course, referring to the other mojo-mechanism in the Finley house—the small black desk with carved talons on its front feet and a pair of wings on its sides. This desk could answer questions . . . if it could be found. Pamela had discovered that when she played a jig on her violin, the desk would come running, eager to dance.

While her mother was busy folding laundry in the kitchen, Pamela led the others upstairs to her bedroom and removed her violin from a case lined with red velvet. She fixed it under her chin, tuned the strings, and rubbed rosin on her bow. While she prepared, the others came up with questions of their own.

"I want to ask if I'm going to be a raven's amicus," said Abby.

"I need to know where disappeared things go," added Gabriel. "And why that robin is after me."

"I have a question, too," said Somes. "About my dad."

Somes rarely talked about his father. Mr. Grindle was a harsh, disagreeable man, and Somes had run away from home several times.

"Somes?" Abby asked gently. "What is it?"

"My dad hurt his hand years ago," Somes explained. "It never healed properly. The pain keeps coming back, and it makes him angry and mean." He shivered. "I asked him once what happened, and he said it was too weird to explain, that I would never believe him. Well, I need to know."

The others nodded in sympathy.

Pamela began playing "Swallowtail Jig." It was a short piece, and she played it over and over in a spirited style. Presently, a clatter came from the downstairs bathroom—as if something was scrambling out of the bathtub. Moments later, a galloping noise came from the staircase. The bedroom door flew open, and the desk made its entry, draped in a shower curtain printed with little goldfish.

The desk did a wild pirouette in the center of the room, flinging metal shower hooks in every direction as it stamped loudly on its carved wooden talons. Then it shook the curtain off, as if to declare itself ready to dance.

Pamela played vigorously. It took ten minutes of fervid dancing before the desk began to wobble with exhaustion. It ended its jig with a high jump, then landed in a crouch on all fours, panting heavily.

Somes had never seen the desk in action before; he kneeled beside it, laughing. "Awesome!" he gasped.

"Okay," said Pamela. "Who wants to ask first?"

"I'll go!" Somes turned to Gabriel. "Will it talk back to me?"

"No," said Gabriel, drawing a key out of his pocket. "If the desk has an answer, it will be lying inside when I unlock it. It might be a thing, or a letter, or—"

"One time," interrupted Abby, "I found a postcard with a picture that came to life."

Somes fixed the desk with a serious look. "A long time ago, when I was a baby," he began, "my dad was driving a truck when something attacked him. He won't tell me what it was, but he lost the tip of his pinkie. It still hurts, twelve years later, and it makes him crazy. So, desk, can you tell me what happened that night?"

"Somes," whispered Abby, "that's a very long question."

"You said it answered questions. What difference does it make if it's short or long?"

Gabriel put the key in the keyhole and turned it, raising the desk lid.

"Look!" cried Pamela.

A glass globe lay in the middle cubbyhole. Little flakes of snow swirled inside it. Somes placed the globe gently in his palm and held it up for the others to see.

Inside the globe, a bakery truck rolled forward out of the blizzard. The words *Love in a Loaf* were painted on the truck's side.

"My dad's bakery truck," murmured Somes.

As the children watched, the driver climbed out and squinted into the falling snow.

"And that's my dad when he was younger."

Mr. Grindle raised the truck's hood to examine the engine. He shook his head and lowered the hood. Suddenly, an enormous black bird swooped down and landed before him. Mr. Grindle stared with astonishment. It was easy to see why, for the bird resembled a raven but with a strangely human head. In addition to wings, it had arms, which cradled a small bundle. Its yellow eyes glared menacingly at the driver.

"Is that a valraven?" murmured Pamela.

"Valravens don't have arms," said Gabriel. "It's Corax— part human, part valraven. Do you see what he's holding?"

"It's a baby!" said Abby with astonishment.

In a swift movement, Corax lurched forward and snapped at Mr. Grindle's hand. Mr. Grindle uttered a soundless cry and nursed his bloody finger. It appeared that Corax had taken something from his victim, which he then dropped from his beak into the mouth of the baby. Then, drawing the baby closer, he spread his wings and flew off into the swirling snow.

Mr. Grindle sank to his knees, clutching his bleeding hand.

Then, very slowly, the truck and Mr. Grindle faded away until nothing remained inside the globe but snow tumbling around in darkness.

Somes didn't say anything for a moment. He simply placed the snow globe back in the desk and shut the lid.

"I can see why my dad didn't want to explain what happened," he muttered at last. "Most people would say he was crazy."

Just then the desk began rattling its talons impatiently on the floorboards, as if to remind the children of their other questions.

Gabriel's turn came next. "How do I find out where my mother is?" he asked.

He turned the key and raised the lid. As he peered inside, his expression fell. There was no slip of paper, no snow globe, nothing in any of the cubbyholes. He was about to close the lid when Abby pointed.

"Ooh! Look in the corner!"

A single feather rested in the third cubbyhole. Gabriel picked it up and turned it over. It was just a fluffy white feather with gray markings, no longer than his thumb. Gabriel held it up to show the others.

"Strange answer," remarked Somes.

"What could it mean?" wondered Gabriel.

"I have no clue," said Abby, rubbing her spectacles.

"Can I go now?" Pamela looked about ready to burst.

Gabriel placed the feather gently in his shirt pocket and closed the lid. "Darn," he said.

Pamela leaned toward the desk. "Deskie?" she whispered. "Where is my father?"

The desk seemed to take a deep breath, but as Gabriel

leaned forward to put the key in the lock, the desk hopped backward.

"Hey!" he said sharply. "Come here!"

The desk crouched and retreated like a dog preparing to flee.

"Why doesn't it want to answer?" Pamela wondered.

Scraping its talons hurriedly on the floor, the desk fled through the gap between Pamela and Somes, thundered down the staircase, and struck the landing with a loud crash.

Moments later, they heard a door slam.

Somes turned to the others. "Well, that's the end of that."

"What about *my* question?" Abby was upset. "I wanted to find out if a raven is going to ask me a riddle on my birthday."

"Hey, look!" said Gabriel.

He pointed to Pamela's window. The robin gazed at them in profile, his eye scrutinizing each child.

"Nobody move," said Gabriel, concerned that a wish was on the way.

At that moment, footsteps came up the stairs. The children turned, expecting that the desk had returned, but when the door opened, it was only Trudy.

"What are you all doing?" she asked brusquely.

Pamela tried to think of an explanation. "Oh, Mom, we're just—"

"Trying not to scare the robin at the window," said Abby.

"What robin?" said Trudy.

The children turned to look.

But Snitcher had flown away.

After his friends had gone, Gabriel headed downstairs to Mr. Finley's study. His father was in his armchair, examining a thick volume with a magnifying glass. He looked weary and frustrated, and simply frowned when Gabriel showed him the feather.

"I have no idea what this means," he said. "I'm sorry."

"Okay, thanks anyway, Dad."

Disappointed, Gabriel trudged slowly upstairs. He passed his aunt's bedroom and noticed that she was applying a brilliant shade of red lipstick. "Are you going somewhere fancy?" he asked.

"Oh no, just meeting a friend." Aunt Jaz took another glance at herself in the mirror, then turned to him. "How do I look?"

There was something different about her appearance. It took Gabriel a moment to realize that she had not applied her little black boomerang eyebrows. Without them, her blue eyes stood out brightly. She looked very nice, and he told her so.

Aunt Jaz's dimples appeared. "Thank you, my dear!" she said. She rose quickly, put on her coat, and said goodbye.

Gabriel continued to his room and sat on his bed, puzzling over the feather. *What can it mean?* he wondered. *What does it have to do with finding disappeared things?*

And then a voice said, *It's quite obvious to me.*

Startled, Gabriel looked up and saw Paladin perched on the bed knob, tidying his feathers very carefully with his beak.

"What's so obvious, Paladin?"

Every raven recognizes a feather like that. It sends chills through his wings. That is a feather no raven wants to see.

"Why? What does it come from?"

A great horned owl.

"Ah!" said Gabriel. He knew that ravens were terrified of great horned owls. And he remembered that he and Paladin had met such owls before.

Do you recall that night in the zoo when the great horned owls entrusted us with the torc? Paladin continued. *They know a lot about its past. If anybody can tell us about disappeared things, it will be them. We must pay them a visit.*

Gabriel gave a sigh. "But I promised my dad that I wouldn't paravolate."

Paladin hopped onto Gabriel's shoulder. *If you learn where your mother is, I think your father will forgive you; he needs your help.*

When his amicus put it that way, Gabriel was convinced. He stood up from his bed and threw the window open. A fresh breeze rippled the curtains.

Paladin hopped to the windowsill, spread his wings, and cried, *Jump!*

❈ The Owls' Secret ❈

The boy and his raven focused their thoughts for a moment, and then Gabriel leaped. He felt his body shiver violently, his arms vanish, his shoulders slide backward to form wings, and his feet shrink into slender talons. It was both terrifying and thrilling, a bit like one's first jump into a deep, dark, and unfamiliar lake. He and Paladin merged into one.

In that instant, they went soaring out the window. Paladin tipped his wings and caught a wind current that raised them high above the Finley house. This was the part about flying that Gabriel loved the most—the sensation of being able to ride the air effortlessly.

Oh, I've missed this so much, he thought.

Borne by a fast current, they flew north over the rooftops of the nighttime city. Cars and taxis crawled in slow, predictable paths below; smoke rose in faint wisps above hundreds of chimneys; the East River glittered beneath the moon like a ribbon of tinsel between Brooklyn and the Bronx. After crossing a small island, they descended over several city blocks toward a dark patch of trees and footpaths.

This was the zoo. It was long after closing time, so there were no keepers on the paths. Gabriel and Paladin glided over the ponds and exhibits until they recognized the building marked BIRDS OF PREY. They perched upon a bench beside the large black glass doors.

Paladin sprang apart from Gabriel, then alighted upon his shoulder and trembled at the prospect of meeting the owls again.

"Remember, we're friends with them," the boy reminded his amicus.

I know, replied Paladin. *But they still give me the shivers. If you don't mind, I would prefer to merge into your body. I don't fancy being an accidental snack for an owl.*

Gabriel agreed that this was a good idea, so Paladin concentrated for a moment and did a leap of his own.

The boy felt a tickle as the raven merged with him. It was a bit like having a very small hand squeeze into the glove you're already wearing—not painful, just very cozy.

All right, Paladin said. *I'm ready.*

Once inside, Gabriel walked past bright displays with photographs of eagles, falcons, and hawks. He didn't stop until he found a door marked NOCTURNAL PREDATORS. The moment he stepped into the room, he felt a sense of danger and the skin on the back of his neck grew prickly. It was too dark to see anything at first, but as his eyes adjusted he recognized the silhouettes of four enormous owls with hornlike feathers on their heads. They seemed asleep, but then their piercing eyes opened and regarded him like a row of judges gazing down at a defendant.

"Who goes there?" said a raspy voice.

"Gabriel Finley."

"The son of Adam Finley?"

"Yes."

"We have been expecting you. You have a lot to explain."

Gabriel was surprised by this ominous greeting.

"Young Finley," said the first owl, "months ago we entrusted you with an ancient torc."

"You were to keep it upon its staff," continued a second owl, "and protect it from all who would use it for evil."

"But you have lost it to a *robin*!" said a third with a shiver of disgust.

"I'm sorry. Really sorry," Gabriel replied.

Their expressions remained unforgiving, and the silence made Gabriel feel ashamed. He tried to explain himself. "I needed to rescue my dad from Aviopolis. You know that he was imprisoned there by my uncle, Corax. When I dueled Corax for the torc, the robin stole it. But I've been trying to—"

"You have no idea how serious the situation is!" interrupted the first owl. "Corax's soul lies trapped inside the torc."

"Wait!" said Gabriel with surprise. "Did you say Corax's *soul* is in the torc? In other words, he's *alive*?"

"Indeed. He commands the robin to do his bidding."

Gabriel felt his stomach turn. "I thought he'd been destroyed," he said. "I've been so stupid. That explains so much. . . ."

"You are in grave danger, all because of your own foolishness," said another owl.

Gabriel wilted in front of his judges. "But I have to find my mother. I'll get the torc back, I promise."

One owl turned skeptically to his neighbor. "Another promise."

"Just one minute!" snapped a plump, scruffy owl at the far end of the perch. "The boy is a good egg. Perhaps his plan is a bit soft-boiled, but better that than rotten or poached, don't you agree?"

Several smaller owls emerged from the shadows and began to cough helplessly—which is how owls laugh.

Hey, Gabriel, said Paladin silently. *That's our friend Caruso. He helped us rescue your father, remember?*

The scruffy owl looked kindly upon Gabriel, and winked at him.

"Thank you, Caruso," Gabriel replied, glad to have one friend in the room.

"This lad dueled a demon double his own diameter," Caruso quipped. "Punned him into purgatory! Riddled him into ridicule! Now the soul of the Lord of Air and Darkness is nailed in the noggin of a nincompoop! The brainpan of a boob! Better he be sealed in a robin's cerebellum than ruling the world, so spare me the gloom and doom and help the lad find his mother."

"How do you propose we do that, Caruso?" replied the first owl.

"Tell him about the *Chamber of Runes*."

The moment Caruso said this, all the owls hushed, then exchanged a flicker of glances, followed by a lot of muttering.

Gabriel grew excited. "Is the Chamber of Runes where my mother is? Is that where the disappeared go?"

"It is a secret place," said the first owl.

"It *was* until Caruso spilled the beans," snapped the second owl.

"All disappeared souls go there," Caruso continued. "The dwarfs who forged the torc created this chamber in the event of a mishap. Anyone who is made to vanish by the torc's magic is separated, body from soul. The soul may wander, but the body becomes captive—"

"Compressed, reduced, and shrunk," quipped a small owl.

"And contained," continued a third owl, "in a stone vessel called a *rune*—and that rune is kept in a place called the Chamber of Runes."

"Where is this chamber?" asked Gabriel.

"Why, deep down in the—"

"SILENCE, Caruso!" interrupted the first owl. "No owl may reveal its location!"

"Why not?" asked Gabriel.

"Corax will seek to free his own body from its rune, then resume his quest to rule the world. Do you realize how many creatures have already been driven to extinction when they refused to serve him? Why, he's killed most of the talking birds in existence—"

"Like who?" asked Gabriel.

"Oh, he's wiped out *hundreds* of species," said Caruso.

"The rapping rheas of Rhodesia and the mumbling moas of Mozambique," said one owl.

"The boasting bustards of Belarus," added another. "The quipsters of Qatar!"

"And perhaps the funniest bird in the world, the Catskill Mountains cuckoo," added a third. "Every gag a winner, every joke a gem."

"None left. And all those punch lines forgotten," intoned another owl, sadly.

"That's nothing compared to what he'll do to you humans," added a stern-voiced owl.

Gabriel turned anxiously from the owl to his scruffy friend. "Please, Caruso," he begged. "I've got to find my mom. I just want my family to be together again." He glanced at the others. "You can all understand that, can't you?"

"I sympathize, dear lad—"

Before Caruso could say another word, the other owls drew in front of him, muffling his voice.

"Young Finley," said the stern owl, "you must return to the mission we gave you. Get the torc from the robin and we will reconsider your request."

* * *

Gabriel left the owls' habitat and strode from the building. Outside, he noticed the full moon. It was bright and magnificent—but it could do nothing to help him bring his mother back.

Paladin sprang free of Gabriel, and hovered before him.

I tell you, he said. *Owls are the absolute opposite of wise. How can they think it's easy to get the torc back from a nasty little bird? This is a catastrophe.*

"Let's just fly home," Gabriel replied.

He jumped, and merged with Paladin. A breeze lifted them above the rooftops and the moon shone down like silver. Then a hopeful thought occurred to Gabriel. *Hey, what if we asked around about this Chamber of Runes? If the owls know about it, maybe some other birds do, too.*

Along their way, they asked some pigeons, who were no help. A laughing gull uttered a brief titter and glided off. Then Paladin spied a proud silhouette perched on the chimney of a very grand house below them. It was a spindly-legged bird with an elegant neck and a long, pointed beak—a stork.

"Good evening!" cried Paladin.

"What's so good about it?" snapped the slender bird.

"The older you get, the lower I get. What am I?" asked Paladin.

The stork gave a dismissive sniff. "You ravens and your riddles."

"Can you guess it?" asked Paladin. "It's simple, really." He waited for the stork to try, but she just perched there. "Okay," he said. "Do you give up? The answer is your voice, because voices always get lower as you get older! Get it?"

The stork drew a long, slow, annoyed breath. "We storks prefer limericks," she replied haughtily.

"Oh, you should have said so," said Paladin. "Listen to this one:

"A man had a nose like a horn.
He played it each morning at dawn,
He needed no feet
To walk any street,
For it ran as he played on his horn."

Paladin laughed, but the stork was unmoved.

"Get it?" said the raven. "He didn't need feet because he had a *runny nose*? It's a pun."

"Not funny," she said. "You can't run with a runny nose."

"You can if you have a sense of humor," the raven grumbled.

The stork looked pleased; she obviously enjoyed feeling superior to him.

Gabriel noticed this, and so he made a suggestion to Paladin. *Ask her about the Chamber of Runes, but say it wrong and let her correct you.*

"Tell me, dear stork," Paladin began. "Have you ever heard of a Hall of Runes, or perhaps it's a Lobby of Runes, or a Parlor of Runes?"

"Tsk, tsk. It's not called any of that," she replied. "Everybody knows it's called the *Chamber* of Runes. Inside it, the runes lie within a circle of fire, and a riddle must be answered for each rune to release the body it contains."

Paladin gave a dramatic sigh. "Well, *obviously*," he said. "The real mystery is where the chamber *is*. Nobody knows that."

"Wrong again," she replied, with a smug glance.

"I'm never wrong," said Paladin (hoping to be wrong).

The stork raised her beak with a supercilious air, and snapped at a floating dandelion seed. "Do you think I'm stupid? I don't tell secrets. I'm not like one of those house sparrows who gossip about everything."

With an awkward slump, the stork descended upon the chimney and tucked her beak into her breast to indicate that there was nothing more to be said.

Paladin gave the stork a humble bow. "Well, thanks anyway," he remarked grimly, before taking off into the air.

Nice try, Paladin, said Gabriel as they gained altitude. *This is hopeless.*

No, not at all! replied Paladin. *She led us to the sparrows. I should have thought of that myself.*

They flew in the direction of Fifth Street. In a short time, they arrived a few houses from the Finley brownstone, where they could hear excited chirruping coming from a tree. Among the branches were hundreds of little stout birds with gray heads and dull brown feathers, eagerly sharing the gossip of the day.

"Greetings, sparrow!" said Paladin to the first house sparrow he saw as he landed on a branch.

"Greetings, raven," answered the sparrow. "What goes?"

Paladin remembered some advice his mother had given him when he was a chick. It was best to offer gossip before asking for some. "Sparrows," she had warned, "are easily offended, but if you're generous with them, they will tell you anything."

"I hear of a robin in these parts who wears a magic necklace," said Paladin.

"Oh, I know that," boasted the sparrow.

"Did you know that he created a blizzard of birdseed?"

"Old news, old news," the sparrow declared, preening her chest.

"Did you hear that he created an earthworm the size of a subway car?"

This startled the sparrow. "Really?"

"And did you know that the spirit of Corax lives inside his necklace?"

"Ooh!" The little bird's dark eyes widened at such a juicy bit of information. Before Paladin could say anything else, the sparrow had jumped to a higher branch. Moments later, the entire tree erupted in a frantic babble of gossip.

"Everybody's talking about Corax, and all because of *me*!" she said as soon as she'd returned.

"Maybe now you could tell me something?" Paladin asked.

"What would you like to know?"

"There's a place called the Chamber of Runes. I wonder where it is."

Nodding vigorously, the sparrow hopped away to consult with her friends. When she returned, she looked about to burst with glee. "I know it!" she said. "It's deep underground, on the outer fringe of Aviopolis to the east."

"Does anyone know how to get there?"

"Oh no. There are lots of rumors, but it's never been found."

Suddenly, the entire population of sparrows converged around Paladin, offering their tidbits of information. "Its location has been lost for centuries." "It's a perilous path to get there." "Not even a raven could find the Chamber of Runes."

Offended, Paladin cast an annoyed glance at the flock. "Well, who does know, then?"

A silence fell upon the group.

"Nobody?"

The sparrows began to chatter among themselves and soon moved on to discussing the best-stocked bird feeders in the neighborhood, and the arrival of a dangerous Chartreux cat on Garfield Place.

With no more to be learned, Paladin flew to the stoop of the Finley house, where Gabriel jumped free of him.

Such irritating birds! remarked Paladin. *"Not even a raven could find the Chamber of Runes." Well, a sparrow couldn't find its own shadow!*

"Don't feel bad," said Gabriel as he beat his arms to get some feeling back in them. "I only wish I'd realized that

Corax's soul was in the torc and that he was commanding the robin."

"I'll bet his body is trapped in a rune, too," added Paladin.

"But he hasn't found it yet, so we must be ahead of him," Gabriel reminded the raven. "At least we know *where* the bodies of the disappeared go; and *what* this place is called; and sort of where the place is. We're so close to finding my mom."

I suppose that is pretty good work for one day, Paladin replied.

This last conversation had carried further than Gabriel realized.

The holly bush in the front yard of the next house stirred slightly after the boy and his raven had gone, and two black eyes peered through the leaves. They belonged to a paunchy robin with a necklace tightly wound around his neck.

"He knows."

Yes, replied the voice in his head. *The Finley boy seems to know a great deal about where my body lies.*

"Eminence?" The robin peered at the soft glow emanating from the windowsill. "I could crush this house into matchsticks, and drive him out right now. Just say the word."

Fool, I warned you once, and I'll say it again. There are some in here who must never be harmed. We shall capture the boy in due time.

❉ Peril ❉

Gabriel, Pamela, and Somes went to Abby's birthday party that Monday evening. Abby greeted them at the door, breathless from having raced down from upstairs. She had a glittery silver boa wrapped around her neck and blinking lights on her pigtails.

"I hope you like Mexican food," she panted. "My mom made my favorite foods tonight: burritos and guacamole. Viv made a carrot cake with strawberry frosting and coconut shavings!"

Viv was Abby's next-oldest sister. Etta, the oldest, was away for a high school trip. Abby's mother came out of the kitchen to greet everybody. Dr. Chastain had a small, friendly, inquisitive face.

"How are things looking these days, Somes?" she inquired. She had prescribed eyeglasses for him a few months earlier.

"Oh, everything looks pretty good, Dr. Chastain." Somes grinned.

Ms. Nash, Abby's other mother, arrived after them. She

was a tall woman with a warm gaze and an elegant gray French braid. She carried a briefcase in one hand, and in the other an enormous brown box, which she lowered carefully to the floor.

"Happy birthday, my sweet," she said. "Have a look at your present."

Abby kissed her, then kneeled down and opened the box. "Oh, Mama," she said. "How did you know?"

"Probably from the stickers you posted on every door of the house for the last month," Ms. Nash replied fondly.

"What'd you get?" asked Pamela.

Abby delicately lifted a glass aquarium out of the box. A small spotted lizard peered from within. "It's an adorable leopard gecko!" she gushed.

After dinner, Abby blew out the candles on her cake, served portions to her friends, and opened her presents. Gabriel gave her a bar of nougat, her favorite candy; Pamela gave her a kazoo; and Somes gave her the most unusual gift of all—a small sculpture of a bird made out of two rusty forks and a spoon twisted together.

"Thanks, guys, I love them," said Abby.

Afterward, the foursome sat in a tight cluster in Abby's living room. Gabriel explained all the things he'd learned about Corax and his mom and the Chamber of Runes.

After they had absorbed the news, Somes spoke up.

"Wait, I don't get it," he said. "Are you able to understand sparrow talk?"

"No," said Gabriel. "But when I merge with Paladin, I seem to understand what other birds say."

Abby uttered a deep sigh.

"What's wrong?" asked Pamela.

"Well, now I'm *twelve!*" she replied. "And I still haven't seen a raven. I just don't think it's going to happen."

Gabriel explained that he hadn't met Paladin until weeks after his birthday. "There's plenty of time," he said.

Abby's shoulders slumped. "I know you're trying to make me feel better, but I think Somes was right. My chances would be much better if I was a Finley."

The next day, Abby was in a better mood. On the way to school, she told Gabriel and Somes that she had decided to name her gecko Gideon.

"Bad name," said Somes. "My dad's name is Gideon. If he's anything like my dad, he'll get annoyed for no reason and snap at you."

Abby felt a pang of sympathy for Somes. "No," she replied as they walked up the steps of Alfred Grimes Academy. "My Gideon has big, friendly eyes and he's very quiet."

"Totally the wrong name," murmured Somes as they merged with the thick crowd of students who filed through the doors.

While the morning bell echoed throughout the building, a line of dark, hooded birds assembled upon the roof. Their thin black feathers were no defense against the wintry breeze. With jaundiced eyes and surly stares, they shivered as they watched the students.

Once they'd taken their seats in math class, Gabriel, Abby, and Somes saw that Mr. Coffin had projected a puzzle on the whiteboard before them:

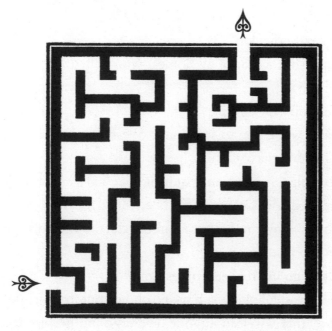

Below it was written a title: *The Riddle of the Maze.*
"I like this guy," said Abby.

"You would," groaned Somes.

Mr. Coffin, his beard tied with three purple ribbons that gave him the distinct appearance of a pirate, paced in front of the room until all the seats were filled, then closed the door.

"As part of our class," he began, "we are going to talk about puzzles. It is my duty to encourage you to stretch your minds. So, who's good at riddles?"

Abby and Gabriel exchanged excited glances, then raised their hands.

"Ah, birds of a feather, eh?" said Mr. Coffin, peering at them. "Anybody else?"

Abby shot a glance at Somes, who rolled his eyes and raised his hand.

"You too, Mr. Grindle?"

"No, I was going to say that it doesn't seem like a riddle to me," said Somes.

"A riddle is a question requiring ingenuity and a sense of fun," replied Mr. Coffin. "This is a riddle for the eyes. The question is: How do you get from the start to the finish without getting lost?"

"Don't go in," replied Somes, smiling.

"Very good. But if you have no choice but to go in, there's one trick that will lead anyone, even a blind person, to the exit."

Gabriel studied the picture, then looked over at Abby,

who shrugged. Finally, he thought about what a blind person would do, and the answer came to him.

"Yes, Mr. Finley?"

"A blind person would follow the wall on the left or the right to get out," said Gabriel.

"Show us," said Mr. Coffin.

Gabriel went up to the board and traced his way along the left wall with a marker. Eventually, he reached the exit.

"Very good, Mr. Finley," said Mr. Coffin. "You've lived up to your famous reputation."

At this, Abby, Somes, and Gabriel shared a baffled glance.

* * *

By the end of school, the entire roof of the Alfred Grimes Academy was lined with black birds—watchful and silent, tattered and unpleasant, beaks open in sinister anticipation.

When the last bell rang, students began to pour out of the main doors.

The birds stirred.

Abby, Somes, and Gabriel dodged clusters of kids and made their way uphill on the tree-lined pavement without noticing the ghouls above them.

"So, what did he mean by your *famous reputation?*" said Abby, who had been puzzling over Mr. Coffin's remark all day.

"Beats me," said Gabriel. "I didn't think he knew anything about me. And what was he saying about birds of a feather?"

"That just means we stick together," said Somes. "I don't trust that dude. And what about when he said we were *connected by magic?*"

"Well, we are, in a way," said Abby. "But how does he know?"

By this time, Gabriel had noticed that the sky had grown dark. It reminded him of when the birdseed blizzard arrived, except there was no magic in the air—just a prickly feeling of some awful threat.

Just then something flew over Gabriel's head, leaving a trail of black feathers like an ugly stain against the sky.

"Duck, Gabriel!" shouted Somes.

Gabriel crouched. A black bird with yellow eyes careered toward him, followed by a dozen others. "Yikes!" he cried.

Talons grabbed his coat collar, more clutched at his hair, and beaks seized his cuffs and backpack straps. A furious tugging commenced as the valravens attempted to pull him into the air.

Desperately, Gabriel swung his arms, windmill-style, to free himself. "Get off me, you freaks!" he screamed.

Somes batted a valraven with his homework binder, sending pages flying in all directions. The fearsome bird circled him, its jagged beak wide in a mocking smile, then it darted at his ear, drawing blood.

Somes clamped his hand to his ear. "Ouch!" he said, but his voice was lost amid the merciless shrieks of the birds.

Abby swung her backpack at a valraven, but another swooped and dug its talons into her scalp.

"Get off!" she hollered.

"Help! They're trying to—" yelled Gabriel, whose feet had left the ground. He fought to get free. "Help!" he shouted again.

Somes grabbed on to Gabriel with both arms, using his weight as ballast to hold him down, but more valravens arrived and began pulling.

Abby finally wrenched off the bird gripping her hair and knocked it away. "Somes, we've got to hit them back!" she cried.

"Hit them? How? I can't reach and I'm the tallest!"

"Wait!" said Abby. With deep, panicked breaths, she pulled something from her backpack—a pair of purple tights.

"Are you going to make the birds wear tights?" Somes shouted.

"Yeah, right," Abby snapped, taking two large baking potatoes from the bag. "These were for an art project at school, but . . ."

She dropped one potato into each leg of the tights and began to swing them in circles until they made a furious humming sound. Then, when the tights were a spinning blur, she hurled them upward.

Poof! Smack! Poof!

Pieces of a valraven shot in all directions—feathers, bones, beak, and gristle whizzed through the air. This had an immediate effect on the other birds, who scattered in terror.

"What was that?" gasped Somes.

"A *boleadora*—cowboys use them in Argentina to catch steers," said Abby.

"Do you have another pair of tights?" asked Somes.

Abby threw her *boleadora* to Somes and dug into her bag again. "Where are the green ones—oh, here!"

She dropped two more potatoes into each leg and swung the tights overhead.

Meanwhile, Somes struck a bird, causing a stunning explosion. A valraven head skimmed across the street like a stone across water.

Abby fired off the next shot and struck a tatty old val-raven that burst apart like a rotten pumpkin, gray flesh splattering upon a No Parking sign while bones clattered to the ground.

The explosions of these phantoms seemed to unnerve the other birds. They dropped Gabriel and fled with frantic cries.

Exhausted, the three kids watched the ghouls retreat over the trees and rooftops, leaving behind a trail of feathers. Gabriel trembled, then sank to his knees.

Somes handed the purple tights back to Abby. "Potatoes and tights," he muttered. "Who'd have thought?"

Abby was busy worrying about Gabriel. She kneeled down beside him. "Are you okay?"

"I'm fine." Gabriel looked at her. "But you're bleeding." He dug into his jacket, drew out a pack of tissues, and dabbed the bloody scratch on her forehead.

At that moment, they both became aware of Somes's lingering gaze.

"I'm bleeding, too, y'know," he said.

"Sorry, Somes," Abby said softly. "Come here, let me see."

Somes showed her his ear. Abby blotted it with a handful of tissues.

"Do you think a valraven's scratch is as bad as a bite from Corax?" Somes asked.

"I doubt it. Why?" asked Abby.

"Well, I keep thinking about the snow globe that showed

my dad being attacked by Corax. He never really healed from that bite."

"We've been scratched by valravens before, in Aviopolis, remember?" Abby stuffed the tights in her backpack and stood. "Let's get cleaned up."

"What did I miss this time?"

Pamela arrived home from school that afternoon to find Gabriel, Abby, and Somes in the kitchen, clean and bandaged—but still shaken.

After they explained about the attack, Pamela kneeled before the stove and whispered a request for hot chocolate. The mojo-mechanism whipped up mugs for everyone in a matter of seconds, and the hot, delicious mixture helped them forget their wounds.

"You know, it's really amazing how you can get that stove and the desk to do whatever you want," Somes said to Pamela. "Who knows what the writing desk might have told you if it hadn't run away."

Pamela shrugged. "Maybe I'm a Finley."

"Well, that could only be if you were related on your dad's—" Gabriel began. "Hey, maybe you *are* related on your dad's side!"

"No way," said Somes.

"Why not?" wondered Abby.

Suddenly, there was a tapping at the window. Paladin was on the sill and hopping excitedly from claw to claw.

Gabriel raised the sash and the raven hopped onto his shoulder. *I just met a nightingale who was at the cemetery late last night. She told me that Snitcher ordered an army of valravens to capture you.*

"They almost did," said Gabriel. "We fought them off on our way home. But what do they want?"

Listen, Gabriel, insisted Paladin. *The nightingale saw Snitcher prove to the valravens that he was carrying the spirit of Corax in the torc around his neck. It's just what the owls told us—the robin is commanded by the Lord of Air and Darkness. And according to the nightingale, the robin heard you talking about the Chamber of Runes. He knows you want to free your mother's body, and believes you can do the same for Corax's.*

Abby, Somes, and Pamela leaned forward, confused because they couldn't hear Paladin's thoughts.

"What, Gabriel? What?" asked Abby.

Gabriel turned to his friends and explained Paladin's news. "But I don't know where this Chamber of Runes is," he continued. "All I know is that it exists . . . somewhere in Aviopolis."

"If Corax is trying to capture you," said Somes, "he must believe you can find it."

"Well, I won't help him." Gabriel folded his arms.

"He sent his valravens to capture you; he'll do it again," Abby said.

"Then we'll fight them off again," said Gabriel.

"Gabriel," said Somes, "get serious. We barely survived that attack. Corax will do anything to get his body back so that he can command his stinking army of birds and—"

"Rule the world," murmured Pamela.

"Don't you dare go outside without us," said Abby.

Gabriel threw up his hands. "First I couldn't paravolate with Paladin, now I can't even walk to school by myself?"

"Just be glad they didn't get you today," said Pamela.

"Get who? What are you talking about?" Trudy was standing in the doorway. Her eyes dropped to the box of bandages on the table. "Honey? Were you hurt?"

"No, I'm fine," said Pamela. "But Gabriel, Somes, and Abby got—"

"Bitten by mosquitoes!" said Abby.

"Good heavens, they must have been enormous," said Trudy.

"And vicious," said Somes. "And it's not even spring."

❀ A Busy Night ❀

For several days Gabriel had intended to tell his father what he had learned about the Chamber of Runes and Corax, but he kept putting it off because he would have to admit that he had paravolated.

You're in far too much danger now, Gabriel, Paladin said. *You must tell him.*

I know, agreed Gabriel. *I'll do it tonight.*

But dinner seemed to go on forever. Adam had made chocolate pudding for dessert, and Trudy took only the tiniest spoonful from her little bowl. "Oh, this is just too much," she said, shaking her head.

"What's wrong with it?" asked Adam.

"It's all that . . . chocolate," she replied with a grimace.

"It's perfect!" said Aunt Jaz, who had been savoring each spoonful. She looked curiously at Trudy. "You used to be crazy about chocolate. Remember when you baked constantly and made those delicious cookies and cakes for all the pastry shops in the neighborhood?"

"That must have been when I was in love," said Trudy. "Chocolate is different when you're in love."

"Hmm. Perhaps it is," said Aunt Jaz softly.

Amused, Gabriel kicked Pamela under the table.

"Mom?" said Pamela. "When did you stop liking chocolate?"

Trudy just sighed.

"Was my dad still around?"

Trudy's eyes darted this way and that, suddenly aware of everyone's curiosity. "I'm sure I can't remember!" she snapped. "Why are you all staring at me?"

Gabriel turned to Aunt Jaz. Though she said nothing, he detected a hint of secrecy in her expression. At once, he felt sure that Aunt Jaz knew something about Trudy's missing memory.

There was no chance to talk to his father in the kitchen. Gabriel helped clear the table and do the dishes, then padded upstairs to find him in the study, already snoring in his big leather armchair. A huge leather-bound volume lay in his lap, open at a page full of confusing Gutnish hieroglyphs.

Gabriel shook his arm. "Dad?" he said, but Mr. Finley continued to snore. Finally, Gabriel gave up and trudged to his bedroom.

When he reached the landing, Pamela looked out the doorway of her bedroom. "Gabriel, can I ask you a question?"

"Sure," he said.

"Did you notice Aunt Jaz just now?"

He nodded. "Yeah, with that weird expression on her face, right?"

"I think it's all connected. My mother, love, chocolate, my dad. Do you know what I think? It's another *Finley secret.*"

Gabriel gave a weary nod. "There are a ton of them."

"She knows something, and I have to find out what."

"How?"

Pamela gave a faint shrug and a smile. "Good night."

When Gabriel entered his room, he saw Paladin sitting on the bed knob. The raven hopped onto his shoulder and nuzzled his ear. A soothing melody from a violin swelled from Pamela's room. Paladin cocked his head to listen.

She plays very well, he remarked.

"Yeah," agreed Gabriel.

If I didn't have you as my amicus, I would choose Pamela.

"Abby would be very sad to hear that," Gabriel replied. "She really wants to bond with a raven."

Paladin rearranged a feather in his left wing, then tucked his beak thoughtfully into his chest. *Finding a raven—or a human—is as tricky as finding a best friend. You can't plan it; you can't predict it; it just happens.*

On this evening full of secrets, there was another meeting going on at the top of Cemetery Hill. Hundreds of dark figures with dim yellow eyes were perched upon every statue and tombstone, waiting to hear a robin speak.

"This is outrageous!" cried Snitcher to the valravens. "Why haven't you brought me the Finley boy?"

The robin paced along the shoulder of a great white statue of an angel. He glanced up at its gentle marble eyes, wishing this heavenly messenger would come to life and take over where the valravens had failed. But the wish was not granted. The torc held no power over angels.

"We almost had him," muttered one valraven.

"How could you possibly fail when there are so many more of you than him?" the robin replied.

"We didn't expect the girl to have such a fearsome weapon," muttered another valraven.

"What weapon?" replied the robin. "You are immortal! Nothing can kill you!"

This question prompted a grudging silence; no valraven would admit that he'd been defeated by potatoes and tights.

The robin's eyes darted back and forth with annoyance. "Can't one of you do what I asked?" he snapped. "Seize the boy when he is unprotected!"

"The best time to catch him would be when he merges with his raven, Paladin," said a gravelly voice. The one-eyed phantom, Hookeye, spoke from his perch upon a mausoleum.

This idea pleased all the valravens. It would be much easier to gang up on a single raven. They uttered *caws* and *throks* of enthusiasm.

"But the boy rarely does that," interrupted the robin. "I

know, because I've watched him for hours through his window. He would only do it if . . ."

The robin looked confused, as if his dim bulb of a brain couldn't manage another thought. But the torc suddenly quivered around his neck, and his voice took on a deeper, more commanding tone.

"He would do it if one of his friends was in grave danger."

"An excellent point, Your Eminence!" said Hookeye, guessing that Corax had found a way to speak through the robin. "The boy cherishes his friends," he remarked with a sneer. "It is one of his weaknesses. Leave the rest to me."

Abby couldn't sleep. Her mind was full of the day's adventure, and she had an uneasy feeling that it was not over yet. A shrill wind made the oak tree outside her window sway and creak. Breezy gusts blew twigs against the sill. The night felt rebellious; it didn't want to settle. She pulled up the blind and peered outside. The waning moon in her backyard cast deep shadows. Then something silky and black fluttered upon her windowsill.

Abby put on her eyeglasses, and raised the window. Standing before her was a black bird with a blunt beak and satin wings. Its bold presence made her giddy with excitement. "A raven?" she gasped. "A raven at my window! Hello!"

It answered her in a deep and raspy voice:

"What has substance but no soul,
Needs neither air nor food
Yet flies in the sky?"

Her heart started to beat faster. *Calm down,* she told herself. And yet it was hard to relax when she knew what this opportunity meant.

"Let me think," she said. But when she looked at the bird, she hesitated.

Ravens are tidy by nature, but this bird's feathers were oddly tattered, and its beak was chipped from age. There was a gaping socket where one eye should have been. Abby couldn't see its other eye because the bird kept its profile to her.

Shame on you, Abby! she thought. *A raven finally invites you to answer its riddle and all you can do is criticize its appearance? It was probably attacked by a hawk or a great horned owl. The poor thing!*

Blinded by desire, she imagined being the raven's *amicus.* This bird would be her friend for life! She would be able to merge with it and fly across the city, coast across cloud prairies, and swoop through billowing white canyons.

"Hmm," she said. "Let's solve this riddle. Whatever this is has a body but no soul. Doesn't need to breathe or eat. Yet it flies. Well, if it doesn't breathe or eat, it can't be alive. . . . Wait a minute, I know what it is!"

She looked at the bird thoughtfully. "My answer is . . . a kite."

As the words left her lips, she had a queasy feeling that her answer was wrong.

The bird turned to face her and revealed its other eye.

It was yellow. A sickly mustard tint. Yellow as bile, as curdled milk, that awful yellow you see in a polluted pond when the edge of the water froths into ghastly bubbles and leaves a vile stain. It was the jaundiced eye of a—

You're a valraven, Abby thought.

You've answered my riddle and opened your mind to me, replied Hookeye. *And until I release you, we are one!*

In a horrible flash Abby felt herself wrenched out of her body and squeezed within the awful, musty, cramped insides of the centuries-old valraven. It was like being buried in a coffin full of dust, ash, and rotten food. She could smell everything the creature had devoured in the last hundred years—mouse skins, rat tails, grubs, beetles, lice and snake flies, maggots, cobwebs, fuzzy blackened fruit, and moldy cheese.

In the next instant, they were hurtling upward. Abby felt nauseated from the stench of the phantom's insides. The higher they flew, the more sickened and revolted she became, but she was determined to keep her wits about her.

Please, Mr. Whatever You Are, she began. *Where are we going?*

To see your friend Gabriel, replied Hookeye.

Why?

Perhaps he'll be moved by your cries to rescue you.

Oh, so that's it. This is all a trap to capture him, said Abby. *Well, I won't do it. I won't say a word; I'm not going to help you trick him.*

You have no choice, my dear, replied Hookeye. *Now that you're inside me, I can use your voice any way I choose.*

❀ The Trap ❀

Gabriel heard a harsh tap on the glass of his bedroom window. He pulled the curtain and saw a valraven's sickly yellow eye staring at him through the pane.

"Paladin!" he called.

The raven flew to his shoulder and peered out. *Gabriel, I remember this phantom. He's Hookeye, Corax's general. A very powerful and dangerous bird.*

"What should we do?" said Gabriel.

Nothing. He's outside and we're inside.

But then Gabriel heard a faint voice.

"Gabriel, it's me, Abby. I'm . . . I'm stuck inside this valraven!"

"Abby?" said Gabriel. "What's going on? Why are you inside a—"

"Never mind," she interrupted. "I did something incredibly stupid. Listen, Gabriel. Whatever happens, don't follow this bird. It's a trap to capture you! Don't follow—"

Hookeye clamped his beak shut, cutting off Abby's words. The old valraven smiled grimly at Gabriel and Paladin, then flew off.

"We've got to follow her," said Gabriel, and he threw up the window and spread his arms, preparing to paravolate.

"But that's exactly what Abby told you *not* to do!" said Paladin.

Gabriel looked at the raven with an anguished expression. "But how can I let Abby be captured?"

Paladin drew a resigned breath. "I understand. It's just that we'd be flying right into—"

"I don't care. *Jump!*" cried Gabriel.

In that instant, Gabriel merged with Paladin, and they took to the air. He felt the wind, thick as water beneath his wings, as they soared in pursuit of the valraven.

Hookeye flew a haphazard course, sometimes ducking beneath tree branches, sometimes gliding into open spaces. Although shrewd, he had the disadvantage of having lost many feathers, so he didn't have the powerful thrust of a younger bird. His wings were sparse and he flapped with great effort. Within half a minute, Paladin had caught up with him.

"Hookeye," he said.

The valraven glared at him. "Ah, Paladin, my friend. And do I have the honor of greeting the Finley boy, too?"

"Let Abby go!" cried Gabriel.

"Oh, don't worry, human," gloated the phantom. "I will— when I'm ready."

"Do it now, Hookeye, or I'll pluck every feather from

your wings until you plummet," Paladin said, and to show that he meant business, the raven dipped in the air and seized one of Hookeye's tail feathers. The valraven gasped.

Abby chimed in now. "Listen to him, you horrible smelly beast! He'll take every feather you've got. If you let me go, you'll still be able to fly, but if you don't, he'll pick at you until you're as naked as a plucked hen!"

Oh, I'll let you go soon, my dear, muttered Hookeye.

"Jump!" Abby said. "Jump! Jump! Jump!" She remembered that Gabriel often said this when he wished to merge with Paladin—or separate. "Jump! Jump!"

Oh, you can say that all you want, but it won't do you any good.

Abby jerked and squirmed inside the valraven's body. "Why can't I get free?" she cried in exasperation.

Because when a human merges with a valraven, it's a surrender, Hookeye replied. *You're my prisoner and you must wait till I release you.*

Abby squirmed again. "I'll scream," she warned. "Aaaaaaahh!"

Hookeye's single, sickly yellow eye grew watery as Abby's shrill cry rattled through his brain. He spiraled down toward a traffic intersection, barely able to alight upon the striped awning of a shop on Union Street printed with the words PLESHETTE'S EXOTICS.

Paladin circled above, looking for a hint of a trap. *I don't see any other valravens,* he told Gabriel.

I guess it's safe, then, Gabriel replied. *But did you notice where we are?*

Pleshette's shop, said Paladin. *That nasty little man who sells potions, animals, and mojo-mechanisms.*

The moment that Paladin alighted on the other end of the awning, a robin fluttered down from a nearby tree and perched between Hookeye and Paladin. *Snitcher!* said Gabriel.

"Ah, so here is Paladin," said the robin. "I presume that the Finley boy is with you?" He gazed with gleeful mischief from Paladin to Hookeye. "Now that I have you both together, let's proceed."

"First," said Paladin, "Hookeye must let the girl go!"

"Very well," said Hookeye. He stretched his wings and gave a vigorous shake.

The figure of a girl with twelve blond pigtails sprang free of the valraven and collapsed upon the pavement. Abby got up, dusted off her pajamas, and adjusted her glasses. The moment she saw the shop window, and the cages inside, she whirled around. "Paladin! Gabriel!" she cried. "Go—"

"Wait!" cried the robin. "Hear me out. If you and the Finley boy tell me where the Chamber of Runes lies, and how Corax can reunite with his body, you may go free."

"Never!" replied Paladin.

"To be trapped and powerless is a miserable existence," said a deeper voice speaking through the robin's mouth. "Show him how it feels, Snitcher."

"I'll never help you, Corax," said Gabriel through Paladin.

A brilliant flash of blue light burst from the torc around Snitcher's neck.

Hey, what's happening to me? cried Paladin. *I can't move my wings or my head!*

Gabriel felt the same sensation, as if they were held in a viselike grip. *Maybe I can jump free,* he said. He attempted a mental jump, but nothing happened.

He tried again. Nothing.

Then Gabriel saw Abby's horrified expression.

"You're in a cage," she said. "It's shaped exactly like a raven, with wire, rivets, spikes, and a metal beak. It's a horrible contraption!"

Paladin squirmed frantically to escape, but the cage held him tight. His desperate movements caused it to fall off the awning and strike the pavement with a clatter.

Abby crouched next to it. "Are you guys okay?"

"We're okay," said Paladin.

She was startled by Paladin's voice; she had longed for the raven to speak to her, but this was an awful time for such a privilege. "I'll carry you home, and get help," she said, but when she tried to pick up the cage, one of her fingers caught on a sharp set of spikes. "Ow!" she cried, flinching.

The cage's metal fastenings were barbed to discourage an outsider from freeing its victim.

"This is terrible," she said.

"Please try to get away before Snitcher harms you," said Paladin.

"But, I can't leave you—"

The cage vanished as Abby spoke.

"What's going on? Where . . ."

A bluish glow emanated from the shop window. Abby peered inside and saw its source. High in the rafters, Paladin's metal cage shone among many others of all shapes and sizes. Then its glow faded and the cage disappeared within the dark interior.

"Gabriel, I'm so sorry," she whispered quietly, as a hot tear rolled down her cheek.

"He'll change his mind soon enough and tell us all we need to free Corax," chirped the robin.

"But he doesn't know anything," Abby wept. "I promise." She wiped her cheeks with her pajama sleeve.

"Oh, calm down," said Hookeye. "Your friend will come to no harm."

Abby glared bitterly at the phantom. "It's a *store*," she replied. "He could be sold by that creepy man."

"Not if he keeps his mouth shut," replied Hookeye. "Nobody wants a silent raven."

She turned to Snitcher. "You know that he'll never help you, don't you?"

"I'll give him a week," replied the robin.

"And then what?" asked Abby.

But Snitcher had already flown away.

❊ Captivity ❊

A bell on the shop door tinkled as its owner, Leon Pleshette, entered. His vast, egglike head was perched on a small, spindly frame. Mr. Pleshette pursed his lips into a mousy sneer as he took off a creased raincoat with loose buttons and hung it on a hook. He donned a green eyeshade and replaced his usual spectacles with a special pair equipped with extra lenses on little extensions.

Cries, hisses, squawks, and squeaks erupted from every corner of the shop. Some cages were shaped like teardrops, others like minarets, but most were rectangles and squares; some were stacked in columns, others bunched in clusters, and still others wedged between boxes. Their captives were of every type: birds, snakes, lizards, mice, hamsters, rats, and crickets. They had one thing in common: they all desperately wanted their freedom.

You might expect the owner of so many animals to be a curious and generous fellow, but Pleshette was a tyrant. As the noises grew louder, the shopkeeper snapped, *"Silence, or you'll all go hungry!"*

The cries hushed to whimpers, but the man waited until they were absolutely silent before he put on a rumpled leather apron and flipped the sign on the door to say OPEN.

Up in the highest rafter—impossible to see amid the disorderly jumble—was the raven-shaped cage.

Gabriel and Paladin had been talking all night about how to escape.

Perhaps we should tell him that we're here? suggested Paladin.

Don't you remember the last time we visited him? Gabriel replied. *He's incredibly greedy; he'd much rather sell you than set you free.*

What if he did sell us? Wouldn't that be better than being here?

We're trapped in a cage sealed with magic, Gabriel reminded Paladin. *If a stranger bought us from Pleshette, we could be stuck inside it forever.*

Okay. In that case, I don't want to be sold, agreed Paladin. *But how do we escape?*

Just then, there was a cry from below.

"Punch! Where are you?" shouted Pleshette.

The shopkeeper was weaving through the cluttered shop, peering inside boxes and under baskets. "It's feeding time, Punch!"

Pleshette stopped at a large brass urn and rapped it with his knuckles. When a high-pitched screech replied, he opened the lid. "Come out, you little rascal."

A small capuchin monkey with a fierce white face and a furry black body popped out. He spat on his hands and arranged the tuft of hair above his forehead into a curl, then glared furiously at Pleshette.

"I was sleeping!" the monkey replied in a shrill jabber. "Why must *I* be the one to feed them?"

A talking monkey? remarked Gabriel.

It doesn't surprise me, Paladin replied. *This is a shop full of unusual things, remember?*

The storekeeper grunted at the monkey. "I can't very well go climbing up there, can I? Get on with it or *you'll* get no breakfast."

Grumbling, the monkey sprang from the urn to a shelf, where he slung a feed bag over his shoulder and grabbed a tiny wooden gavel. Then he leaped up to the cage of a cockatoo, struck the bars with a gleeful *rat-a-tat-tat,* and flung out a handful of gray pellets.

The elegant white bird dodged the angry rain of food.

"Stupid! Stupid! Stupid!" Punch murmured in a high, careless tone. "You're all stupid. That's why you're here!" He giggled and swung to the next cage.

Using his tail to anchor himself, the monkey made his way up the tower of cages, leering at mice, rats, snakes, and birds of all sizes, flinging pellets of food into each cage, then striking the bars with his gavel. "Wake up, stupid! Not one of you is as smart as Punch!"

When Punch reached the ceiling, he swung deftly from one hanging cage to the next, tossing birdseed and rattling each cage till its inhabitant cowered and shrank from him.

What a little monster, said Gabriel.

What's he going to do when he sees us? asked Paladin.

When the monkey had worked his way to the top rafters, he stopped suddenly. His eyes narrowed as he examined the peculiar cage with its network of rivets and metal fastenings. He cocked his head with curiosity.

"A raven? Ravens are supposed to be very intelligent," said Punch.

"We are," Paladin answered.

The monkey smirked. "Okay, stupid, let's see what you can do. I've heard your kind loves riddles. Answer me this:

"I'm the ruler of you all—
Feather, bubble, cannonball.
That which rises shall soon fall.
None on earth resist my call."

Punch revealed a cunning smile. "What am I?"

"*Feather, bubble, cannonball,*" thought Paladin. *Those are odd choices. They all fall through the air differently.*

This riddle is about things that fall, added Gabriel. "*None on earth resist my call.*" . . . *Well, why does everything on earth fall?*

"This ruler's name must be . . . gravity!" said Paladin.

Punch wrinkled his nose and frowned. "Who told you?" he snapped, glaring at the other creatures. "One of you? Speak up!"

"No one told me," Paladin replied. "I solved it."

"Liar!" The monkey began striking the cage with the gavel. "Liar, liar, liar! No food for you, liar!"

"What are you doing up there, Punch?" shouted Pleshette. "Don't you want your breakfast?"

The monkey spun the cage with a last whack of the gavel. He swung down to the counter and joined Pleshette, who handed him a banana.

How long do you think we'll last before we starve to death? wondered Paladin.

The cage trembled as the boy and the raven imagined this bleak ending to their lives.

The next morning, Trudy Baskin came downstairs to find Adam, Aunt Jaz, Pamela, Somes, and Abby at the breakfast table. "Goodness," she said with surprise. "So many visitors on a school day."

"Oh, it's okay, Mom," said Pamela. "I invited them here for popovers."

Trudy looked puzzled. "You made popovers? They're not easy. In fact, they're quite . . ."

Pamela pointed to the stove, where steam rose in little curlicues from a cluster of golden pastries.

"Help yourself," said Mr. Finley.

"No time," said Trudy. "Pamela, I have a dentist appointment, so I won't be riding with you on the train."

But she didn't leave without noticing Gabriel's absence. "Where is he?" she asked.

"Sick," said Abby. "Brushing his teeth," said Pamela. "In the shower," said Somes, all three at the same time.

They shared a nervous glance; then Pamela said, "Gabriel's sick, and he's brushing his teeth while he takes a shower. . . ."

"Annoying boy," said Trudy. She threw on her coat. "Don't be late for school, dear!"

"Sure, Mom," said Pamela.

After Trudy's exit, the stove gave a hiss of relief. Its metal arm sprang to the oven door to rescue a fresh batch of popovers, which it dropped with a clatter on the griddle.

"So you saw the cage inside Pleshette's shop?" said Mr. Finley, focusing his gaze on Abby.

"Yes, and the robin and the valraven flew off after that," Abby replied.

"Snitcher?" said Mr. Finley. "The robin who wears the torc?"

"Right, with Corax inside it telling him what to do," added Somes.

Mr. Finley gave a deep sigh. "Let me just go over what we know so far. People who disappear through the torc's magic are split, soul from body. The body is trapped in some sort of small vessel or rune, surrounded by a ring of fire. And these vessels lie in a place called the Chamber of Runes?"

"Exactly," said Abby. "That's everything the stork told Gabriel."

"But I thought there was something else," said Pamela. "I can't remember. . . ."

"Where is this chamber?" said Mr. Finley.

"The sparrows told Paladin it was deep underground, somewhere east of Aviopolis," said Pamela.

"But Corax doesn't know that, because Gabriel wouldn't tell," said Abby.

"Corax must be quite confident that Pleshette won't notice the extra cage," said Mr. Finley. "If Pleshette had a clue what Gabriel has found out, you can be sure he would strike a deal with Corax. We must hope that the shopkeeper remains ignorant about the cage."

"The poor things," fretted Aunt Jaz. "To be trapped inside such an awful place."

"I'm going to go over there right now to talk to Pleshette," said Mr. Finley.

"Can I come?" asked Pamela.

"Me too?" said Abby and Somes quickly.

Adam folded his hands. "I believe you're the best friends anyone could have," he replied. "But school comes first. Off you go!"

At Pleshette's shop, a steady stream of customers had been coming in to browse his wares. They studied the dozens of unusual cages hanging overhead, the jars of powders and liquids, and the peculiar amulets and stones in the glass display beneath his cash register. Leon Pleshette ignored most of them. He studied his newspaper or filled in the crossword puzzle, answering their occasional questions with a sniff or a sneer, or an irritable retort like "Get out!"

Gabriel wasn't surprised to see most visitors leave without buying anything, although he wondered how Pleshette stayed in business.

The answer arrived when a shady-looking fellow in an overcoat entered. Looking around suspiciously, he said, "I'm trying to find . . . *Obedience Powder.*"

Pleshette dropped his paper, flipped the sign on the door to CLOSED, and greeted his visitor with unusual courtesy. "Very good, sir," he said. "For children or adults?"

The man cast another glance around. "What's the difference?"

"For children it comes in lemonade flavor. Mixed with water, it'll make them do anything you say for about an hour," said Pleshette. "Good for dentists and nervous babysitters. Of course, if you need it for adults, I have coffee flavor. My best customers are used-car dealers. You can sell any junkyard wreck to a customer who drinks this. Finally, I have flavorless Obedience Powder, which costs a bit more."

"Flavorless?"

"Mix it in cookie batter, or sprinkle on a cracker, or stir into the water dispenser. Serve it to supermarket customers and tell them to buy all the rotting fruit and out-of-date meat. Very popular at flea markets for selling odd socks, shirts that don't fit, dud lightbulbs, dead batteries, broken radios. Pays for itself in savings!"

After the customer left with three boxes of flavorless Obedience Powder, there were several others who came in— each shiftier and more peculiar than the last.

An elderly woman wearing intensely dark mascara, large brass hoop earrings, and a shawl asked for Clairvoyance Candies. She bought four bags. Pleshette handed her a receipt with a smile.

"Until next month, Madame Valentino?"

Popping a candy into her mouth, Madame Valentino widened her eyes and shook her head. "No, my dear. I predict we shall soon pass each other on Bleecker Street on a dark and stormy night."

Pleshette didn't seem convinced, but he nodded. "Very well, then."

Do you think they really work? Paladin wondered.

As well as Magic 8-Balls and rabbit's feet and stuff like that, I bet, Gabriel replied. *I doubt anything Pleshette sells can be trusted.*

Two men entered the shop, looking for a creature called a Lottery Lizard.

Mr. Pleshette ordered Punch to retrieve a cage containing a small orange lizard with a slithering tongue and bulbous black eyes.

"Your chances of winning the grand prize in a lottery are

one in thirteen million," said Pleshette. "But with my little friend here, you'll be tomorrow's winner!"

He laid a blank lottery ticket on the counter and placed the lizard on top of it. The creature darted about the card, marking holes in some of the numbers with the tip of one claw. When it had picked six numbers, Pleshette held up the card to show the two men.

One man leaned forward to read the numbers, but Pleshette flipped the card so that they couldn't be seen. "Not so fast," he said. "My Lottery Lizards are never wrong, and I'm not in this for my health. Little Rufus here is worth five thousand dollars at least."

Paladin and Gabriel listened to the customers haggle about the price.

I doubt those lizards work, remarked Gabriel. *If they did, Pleshette could just close his shop and make all the money he wants playing the lottery. I bet those customers come back to complain and he makes some excuse about the lizard not being fed properly.*

After the deal was done, Pleshette saw his customers to the door just as a new one entered. Bearded, in a corduroy jacket, he had a scholarly appearance. "Good morning," he said. "I'm looking for something very unusual. It's a raven in a metal cage about this size. . . ."

Paladin! said Gabriel with surprise. *That sounds like my dad.*

Up in the rafters, the raven peered through the eyeholes of his wire prison, trembling with hope.

Adam Finley gestured with his hands, to show the size of

the cage. Pleshette looked puzzled. "I have nothing like that here."

"You haven't even looked."

"Don't need to," said Pleshette. "I know what's in my shop. Leave your name and number. I'll call if one turns up."

Mr. Finley handed him a card, and Pleshette studied the name. "Adam Finley? I know you. You bought a stove years ago—the one that made potions. A very valuable piece of—"

"Listen, Pleshette," Mr. Finley interrupted. "I'll trade you the stove for the raven. Look for him. Now!"

Pleshette folded his arms. "I know what I have. And I don't have it."

Frustrated, Mr. Finley peered up at the jumble of items hanging from the ceiling. "Paladin!" he cried. "I've come to set you free!"

"I'm here!" answered Paladin.

But the moment the raven spoke, twenty other birds joined in, hoping to be rescued.

"I'm here!" repeated five mynah birds.

"I'm here! I'm here!" cried a dozen budgies and parakeets.

"I'm here! I'm here! I'm here!" cried the African gray parrots, the blue-fronted Amazons, and the Indian ringnecks. Each bird cried louder than the one before.

Paladin tried again. "No, I mean, I'm Paladin!"

"No, I'm Paladin!" repeated the budgies.

"I'm Paladin!" mimicked the Quaker parakeets.

"No, I'm Paladin!" added a cockatoo, not to be outdone.

"*Paladin, Paladin, Paladin!*" cried a king parrot. And to make it even more confusing, a macaw followed this by emitting a piercing shriek that rattled everybody's ears.

As every creature in the shop shrieked for Mr. Finley's attention, Pleshette turned crimson with rage. "*Punch!*" he shouted.

The monkey sprang up the tower of cages, striking as many of them as he could with his gavel. When he got to the ceiling, he flipped the gavel around and poked its handle through the wires of Paladin's cage, jabbing the raven painfully in the chest.

"Don't be stupid, stupid, stupid," he warned.

"You have a lot of unhappy creatures," Mr. Finley told Pleshette.

"Oh, they just like attention." Pleshette's eyes probed his visitor. "This raven must be *exceedingly* valuable to you, Mr. Finley. Why, I wonder?"

"It's a family matter," Adam replied as he scrutinized each cage hanging above—and each desperate captive. But though Abby had described the unusual cage *and* its location near the ceiling, he couldn't see past the junk strung from the rafters. In fact, it seemed that the shopkeeper disposed of his garbage by hanging it up rather than discarding it.

Disappointed, Adam turned to Pleshette. "Yes, he is

exceedingly valuable. I advise you to check your stock and be sure to call me immediately when you locate him."

Pleshette tucked the card into his pocket. "Certainly. A raven called Paladin?"

"Yes."

The moment Mr. Finley was out the door, Pleshette stared up into the rafters and began counting the cages.

"Eighteen, nineteen, twenty . . ."

The mischievous monkey slowly lowered the gavel from Paladin's neck. "'Exceedingly valuable,'" he repeated in a whisper. "What can Punch get for Paladin, I wonder?"

Peering down at his master, the mischievous monkey began interrupting the shopkeeper's tally with wrong numbers.

"Seventeen."

"*Fifteen!*"

"Eighteen."

"*Sixteen!*"

Pleshette threw up his hands. "How am I supposed to count my cages with you babbling away? Is it possible I've a raven that I don't know about?"

Punch folded one little hand beneath his chin with artful innocence. "Oh no, no ravens up here."

"I didn't think so," sighed Pleshette. "Just another person trying to waste my time."

The monkey glanced slyly at his master and whispered softly, "Stupid, stupid, stupid."

❈ The Raven's Amicus ❈

Trudy prepared a meal that evening with a very unappetizing name: turkey gizzard casserole. While she crashed pots and pans together in the kitchen, Mr. Finley had a serious conversation with Abby, Pamela, and Somes in his study.

"I didn't see the cage," he said. "And Pleshette doesn't seem to know he has it. The shop is a chaotic mess."

"What if Pleshette doesn't find him?" asked Abby.

Mr. Finley shrugged. "Leon Pleshette always regretted selling the stove to me; he'd love to get it back for nothing. I suspect that if he gives up looking for Paladin today, his greed will drive him to resume the search tomorrow."

At that moment, Trudy gave a shrill cry from downstairs: "Dinner's ready!"

Mr. Finley sighed at the thought of Trudy's cooking. "Care to join us for turkey gizzard casserole?"

"*Turkey gizzard?*" Somes looked horrified.

Pamela, however, glanced at the door and whispered, "When Mom wasn't looking, I asked the stove to fix it up. I promise it'll be *delicious.*"

Somes called home and got his dad's permission. Abby dashed across the street to tell her mothers that she would be eating at the Finleys'.

When everybody had gathered in the kitchen to help set the table, they were overwhelmed by the wonderful smell coming from the oven.

Trudy was puzzled. "I smell nutmeg and paprika," she said. "But I didn't *use* nutmeg and paprika."

The casserole glowed golden brown, with little puddles of butter and wisps of steam rising from the surface.

Trudy served helpings to Mr. Finley, Aunt Jaz, and the children, then took her first forkful and gasped. "I've never made something so delicious in my life," she said.

Pamela shared a secret smile with Somes and Abby.

Aunt Jaz, however, looked rather upset. Her eyes settled upon the one empty table setting, where Gabriel would have sat.

"Oh!" said Trudy, following her glance. "I forgot Gabriel! He doesn't generally enjoy my cooking, but I must take a serving up to him—"

"I'll do that," said Pamela quickly.

"Don't go too close, dear. He might be contagious," said Trudy. "It's probably something he caught from that dirty raven."

Pamela gathered a napkin, silverware, and a plate of food, then hurried upstairs to Gabriel's bedroom. It was empty, of course. The window sash was still open from his attempt to rescue Abby the night before.

Pamela decided to eat his serving so that she could take the emptied plate back downstairs. She closed the window and sat on the bed. The casserole was delicious, but when she had finished her last bite, she heard a voice.

Where is Paladin?

Who's that? she wondered, staring at the window. There was no one to be seen.

Where is Paladin? the voice repeated. *Is he safe?*

Pamela hadn't forgotten about Abby's terrible encounter with Hookeye. But this voice felt so close, so familiar and friendly, that she drew nearer and raised the window. "My name is Pamela," she replied. "Paladin is in trouble. He was captured and put in a cage. Who are you?"

I am Vyka. I'm his friend.

Pamela suddenly realized that she was hearing the voice in her head. And this, she remembered, was a sure sign of a special encounter with a raven.

A bird landed upon the windowsill. Her dark satin feathers caught the light and radiated a deep blue sheen. She was the most beautiful raven Pamela had ever seen.

The two looked at each other for a long moment, and then the raven recited a riddle: *"What question can never be answered with yes?"*

Pamela felt a shiver. She had been asked a riddle by a raven!

Concentrating, she imagined the possible answers. *Any question can be answered with yes, though it may not be correct*, she thought. This was tricky. So the only question that can't be answered is one asked of someone who is unable to reply.

It was then that she guessed the answer. "I know," she said. "The question that can never be answered with yes is 'Are you dead?'"

The raven laughed—a silvery giggle so sweet and clear that Pamela almost wept. Then the raven bowed to her.

Will you be my amicus? asked Vyka.

Later, when Pamela returned with the empty plate, all eyes turned to her.

"Goodness, he ate everything!" said Trudy with surprise. "He's never done that before. Perhaps he's not as sick as you think. Sit down and have your dinner now, dear."

"But I just—" But then Pamela thought better of her reply and drew the full plate toward her.

After dinner, Pamela led Abby and Somes out of the house. "Guess what?" she said on the stoop. "I answered a raven's riddle while I was upstairs!"

Abby's smile faded. "You did?"

"I did. She's beautiful, and her name is Vyka," Pamela explained.

Abby's mouth dropped open. "Pamela," she said, *"I hate you!"*

Without another word, she stood up to leave. Somes

caught her by the arm. "Abby, c'mon," he said. "That's not nice. This is good news."

"Why?" snapped Abby, trembling with fury.

"Maybe she can help us rescue Gabriel."

Abby stopped. She turned and glared bitterly at Pamela. "Pleshette hates children. He'd never even let us into his store."

"He will if we offer to sell him a talking raven," said Somes.

"But we won't actually do it," added Pamela hastily. "That'll be our way to get in."

"Oh, really?" snapped Abby. "And then how do we get Gabriel free? It's impossible. He's in a cage with a *melody lock*. You need a robin to open it. Don't you see how hopeless it is?"

At first, Pamela was stunned into silence by Abby's anger, but then she spoke. "Right, a melody lock! Remember when we went to Aviopolis to rescue Gabriel's father? And we found a room full of ravens trapped in those bird-shaped cages?"

"That's right, I remember," continued Somes. "Pamela opened them by playing a robin's song on her violin."

Abby's harsh expression melted and tears rolled down her cheeks. "God, I'm so awful, Pamela." She licked her glasses and dried them on the hem of her dress. "Look, I don't hate you, but if you hate me for being such a brat, I'll understand."

"I don't hate you, stupid," Pamela replied. "We'll go rescue Gabriel tomorrow right after school."

As Pamela, Abby, and Somes parted ways, they felt a giddy mix of relief and excitement. Abby was glad to have friends who forgave her so quickly. Somes was pleased to have thought of a plan to get into Pleshette's shop. But Pamela had the most complicated feelings of all: a raven had asked her a riddle. Did it mean she was phenomenally lucky? Or did it mean—and this was something both troubling and puzzling—that her father was a Finley?

❈ Second Day in the Cage ❈

There wasn't much for Paladin and Gabriel to do but sleep until Punch made his morning rounds. The monkey had artfully concealed the metal cage from Pleshette's view with hanging carpets. In fact, this little hideaway seemed to contain a number of items Punch reserved for himself—an immense sack of red pistachio nuts, some boiled eggs in a string bag, and a clear plastic purse containing an array of multicolored scrunchies for the tuft on his head. At feeding time, he hammered the cage with his gavel until they awoke, then poked a few gray pellets through the metal beak into Paladin's mouth. "Eat! Eat!" the monkey screeched.

The pellets tasted as dull and dry as sawdust. Revolted, Paladin spat them out.

"Must eat!" Punch leered. "You're a valuable raven, and only Punch will feed you."

I think we'd better do what the monkey says, Paladin, said Gabriel. *Anyway, I'm starving.*

I wish I could eat his tail for breakfast.

So they ate, and then sank back into a gloomy half-sleep, vaguely conscious of the activity in the shop below.

Visitors to Pleshette's shop fell into two categories: There were the puzzled browsers who didn't see anything useful and left after a minute or two. Then came the *real* customers—sneaky types who entered wearing sunglasses and hats that concealed their faces—who requested all kinds of odd concoctions, from Lucky Lozenges (for gamblers to improve their winnings) to Contagious Cologne (a perfume that compels people to mimic the person wearing it).

"Comedians and politicians are my best customers for this product," said Pleshette. "If you laugh, everybody else who smells the scent will laugh. If you clap, applause will break out. Just don't run to the bathroom or you'll cause a stampede."

Some customers bought Phone Parrots (who could talk in any voice, for keeping up a phone conversation while you lie down and take a nap) or Quiz Mice (who sit in your top pocket and whisper the answers to test questions).

Gabriel and Paladin noticed that Pleshette told every customer that his products did marvelous things, but his guarantees sounded slippery. "If it doesn't work, I'll give you something else of equal value," he promised.

Around noon, a familiar voice woke them out of their daze.

"Good morning, my good man!" A tall gentleman with white hair and a weather-beaten face had entered. He wore a tweed coat with a stylish maroon silk scarf knotted around his neck. A gray raven perched on his shoulder.

"Septimus Geiger at your service," he said. "I have some items that may be of interest to you, Pleshette. But before we begin I shall require a cup of tea with cream and sugar, and my raven, Burbage, would appreciate a small white mouse."

Pleshette glanced at the visitor, then at the gray bird. "Didn't you used to have a white raven?"

"Yes, old Crawfin," said Septimus. "He came to an unfortunate end, disappeared by magic, poor fellow. This is his brother, Burbage."

The raven dipped his head and said, "Make that *two* mice, if you please. Fresh, not frozen."

"How long has it been, Septimus?" said Pleshette. "Was it last year when I introduced you to that little troublemaker, Gabriel Finley?"

Gabriel's ears pricked up. *Hey, Paladin,* he said. *It's Septimus Geiger! Remember him?*

Of course I do, replied Paladin. *How could I forget how that weasel stole the torc from you, but was so tormented by its mischievous black magic that he gave it back? Then he helped us rescue your father from the citadel in Aviopolis. He must be here to sell something to Pleshette. I wonder if it's bought, borrowed, or stolen.*

Pleshette flipped the sign on his door to read CLOSED and brought out two teacups. "Punch!" he cried. "Fetch me a couple of mice, pronto."

The monkey emerged from his brass urn, swung up to

a cage, and extracted two live mice by their tails. He teased Septimus's raven by dangling the first mouse a few inches beyond his reach.

Burbage snapped at it—but missed.

"Stupid, stupid, stupid!" cackled the monkey, and he swung the mouse before the raven again.

The gray raven darted forward, ignoring the mouse, and bit the monkey's tail.

"*Aaaaeeeiii!*" Punch released both mice and the raven swallowed them in two snaps.

"Good heavens, what an unnecessary fuss!" shouted Septimus.

The terrified monkey swung up to the rafters and nursed his tail, sobbing to himself, "Stupid, stupid, stupid!"

Pleshette ignored the monkey's weeping. "What brings you here, Septimus?"

"I've been underground."

The shopkeeper's eyes narrowed. "Aviopolis?"

When Septimus nodded, Pleshette darted to the window and drew down the blind. Then he turned to a beautiful blue enamel and silver samovar on the shelf and whispered, "Tea, *pozhaluista*"—*please* in Russian.

The samovar uttered a baritone sigh; then its stubby brass legs quivered to life and trotted over to the cups. The faucet gasped and poured hot water into each cup. Then the elegant little teapot on top of the samovar scuttled down to add tea to the cups and sprang back to its perch.

Septimus scrutinized his cup. "A little more, please?"

Muttering *"Zhadnaya"*—*greedy*—the teapot dispensed more tea.

From the rafters, the captives peered down with great interest.

Paladin? said Gabriel, excited. *Should we try to get Septimus's attention? He might help us.*

Have you forgotten how the parrots drowned me out when your father came? said Paladin.

Oh, right, said Gabriel.

"And what did you find underground, Septimus?" continued Pleshette.

"Well, you may recall that the city of Aviopolis was all but destroyed during the defeat of Corax," he said. "The citadel collapsed, the great chambers were smashed to rubble, and the Finley boy chased after the robin who stole the torc."

"Spare me the history lesson," said Pleshette. "Did you find anything for me to *sell?*"

"Certainly, my dear fellow." Septimus nodded at a rumpled leather drawstring bag at his feet. Pleshette reached for it, but Burbage snapped at his fingers. The shopkeeper drew back, giving the raven a dirty look.

"As I was saying," continued Septimus. "Burbage and I went back there to try to find items of value."

"And?"

"You may recall that Aviopolis was built by dwarfs—

masters of the forge—who created mysterious jewels of gold or silver that were charmed with black magic."

"Yes, yes?" said Pleshette, his eyes focused on the bag.

"Well, we wandered to the east for what seemed like miles until we came to a maze. After we made our way through it, we discovered a pair of doors. Naturally, I was curious about what lay beyond them. So I used my extraordinary wits and consummate skill to unlock—"

"But *mostly* an ax," added Burbage.

Septimus glared at the raven. "It's *my* story, Mr. Smarty-Pants. Let me tell it my way. Anyway, I entered to see a chamber with a pedestal rimmed by—"

"*What's in the bag?*" said Pleshette impatiently.

Annoyed by this second interruption, Septimus stopped talking and slowly dabbed his forehead with a handkerchief. "A pedestal rimmed by fire, which contained . . ." He paused. "May I have a spot more tea?"

Pleshette stamped his foot. "In the name of Nellie Bly, Septimus!" he said. "Will you forget the tea and explain what's in the bag?"

Septimus widened his eyes. "*Amazing* things. See for yourself." He began to loosen the drawstrings on the bag. "Stand back!"

Overhead, Paladin peered through the eyeholes of his cage. Every creature in the shop seemed in suspense, anxious to know what had been retrieved from the ruins of Aviopolis.

With a flourish, Septimus revealed his prize.

Pleshette's expression dropped, and he sank back in his chair. "Four rocks? Very funny, Septimus."

But the light in his guest's eyes remained bright.

"These are *runes*, my friend. They contain unfortunate captives—shrunk down, of course—who disappeared when the torc's magic was cast upon them."

Gabriel felt his heart start galloping. *Paladin! Septimus found the Chamber of Runes!*

As Septimus explained the significance of his discovery, Pleshette offered him a cigar. Presently, a billowing cloud of orange smoke filled the shop and the room began to smell like sweaty socks and boiled cabbage mixed together.

"Galimpong cigars. They're made from the—*hic!*—of a yak," said Pleshette, hiccuping helplessly.

"What?" replied Septimus. "What part of a yak are they made from?"

"The—*hic!*—of a yak."

Even though it was impossible to know what part of a yak Pleshette was referring to, Septimus grimaced at the cigar and stubbed it out. "Look here, man, let's talk about how much these runes are worth."

"Very well," said Pleshette. "I'll give you twenty bucks for the lot of them."

"Nonsense," said Septimus. "My dear fellow, these runes are worth thousands each."

Pleshette laughed. "Thousands for a stone! You're cracked, crocked, and cockled!"

"Wait." Septimus carefully picked out one stone and lit a match behind it. "Take a closer look, my friend."

Pleshette folded down one of the thickest lenses from his peculiar spectacles, and peered at the peach-sized rock with the light glowing behind it. "Good heavens!" he cried.

There was something inside—and it moved.

"P. T. Barnum's holy trousers," whispered Pleshette. "Perhaps these *are* runes."

"Precisely!" chuckled Septimus. He blew out the match, then glanced at his raven. "Hey there, Burbage. Please stop that."

"Stop what?" answered Burbage innocently. He was perched beside a cage marked QUIZ MICE. A mouse tail had just disappeared into his beak. The cage's little wire door hung open and mice were leaping out to save their lives.

"Don't eat the merchandise," snapped the shopkeeper, waving the raven away from the cage and locking it. He returned to the counter, where he drew a small mineral hammer from a drawer. "Now, how does one release the contents of a rune?"

As Pleshette began tapping at the unusual stone, the figure inside turned abruptly and peered out.

"I—I—I wouldn't do that," stammered Septimus. "It's very delicate."

"How else do you get it out?" retorted Pleshette, tapping harder.

He tapped two more times, and a blinding blue light enveloped the room followed by a shattering noise, as if a thousand windowpanes had been smashed at the same moment.

"Oh dear," said Septimus.

A dwarf-sized man stood where the rock had been on the counter. He had a fearsome glare on his face, and an enormous red beard that sprayed out in all directions.

He shouted at Septimus. "Ske-dig-dig-digga? Ske-dig-dig-digga? Felogghabbad!"

"Greetings, my, um, friend!" cried Septimus. He offered his cigar.

The dwarf, however, was glaring at Pleshette, who held up his tiny hammer as if to protect himself.

The dwarf eyed the hammer and drew an enormous sword from his scabbard, preparing to swing, but then his expression changed. He groaned, lowered his sword, clutched his belly, and stiffened. Then, quite abruptly, he burst into a million brilliant pieces, which fizzled into thin air.

A smell of rotten eggs filled the room. Cinders fluttered down upon the counter. Burbage shook his feathers. Septimus and Pleshette coughed and patted themselves off.

"You owe me . . . thousands!" gasped Septimus.

"I'm not paying for that one." Pleshette sniffed. "They shouldn't explode."

"Oh, you're an expert on runes all of a sudden?" said Burbage sarcastically.

"I don't see the value of these things," Pleshette argued. "Who would buy a dwarf waving a sword? It's not something you want in your living room."

"You're missing the point," said Septimus. "Each rune contains the victim of a wish granted by the *torc*."

"A torc that grants wishes—now, *that's* something I would buy," Pleshette mused. "But I don't see any use for a rune."

"And if I told you that the Lord of Air and Darkness is trapped in one?"

"Corax?" Pleshette turned pale, but then a greedy smile formed on his lips. "Well—that could bring *millions*. May I see it?"

Septimus received a cautionary glance from the gray raven and drew the bag close to his chest. "I can assure you, he's here, along with two others," he replied. "One contains my old raven, Crawfin—Burbage's brother. The third contains a woman, I think. I don't know who she is."

Paladin! said Gabriel. *It must be my mother! The owls told us she was in the Chamber of Runes, and these runes hold victims of the torc's magic. Septimus found her.*

The question is, replied Paladin, *would he help you release her?*

Down below, Septimus had just asked Pleshette to show him the millions he would pay for Corax's rune.

"Who keeps that much money lying around?" the shopkeeper protested. "I would need to make arrangements." His expression grew cautious. "But this rune isn't worth anything unless you can get Corax out of it without it exploding into smithereens."

Septimus frowned. "Clearly, your hammer was the wrong approach. I happen to know someone who might know. He's an expert on the torc's history. Professor Adam Finley."

In the cage above, Gabriel ached with frustration. *If only we could escape now,* he said to Paladin. *I could free her.*

How? replied Paladin.

Don't you remember? The stork told us that you need to answer a riddle to release a rune's captive.

Pleshette picked up Adam Finley's card from the counter. "Interesting," he murmured. "Finley was just here, looking for a raven called Paladin."

Septimus glanced up at the cages. "Gabriel Finley's raven?"

Gabriel decided this was his chance. "Septimus!" he cried. "It's me, Gabriel!"

"Septimus, Septimus, Septimus!" cried the parrots.

"It's me! It's me! It's me!" cried the cockatoos.

"Gabriel! Gabriel! Gabriel!" cried the mynahs.

Punch swung over and hammered the gavel against the cage until Paladin uttered a gasp of pain.

"Is Gabriel here?" said Septimus.

The noise in the shop was deafening as every bird claimed to be Gabriel.

Pleshette flipped up his green visor and shook his head at

Septimus. "No, they're only repeating words they've heard. They're just stupid birds." Pleshette stole another glance at the bag of runes. "Why don't you leave that with me and invite the professor over for a chat?"

"I've got a better idea," replied Septimus. "I'll keep the bag until you come up with a bundle of cash to buy the runes."

Pleshette became annoyed. "Now, look here, you didn't have a clue what Corax's rune was worth until you came to me. How do I know you won't strike up some shady deal and sell it to this professor?"

The two men glared back and forth for a moment, neither trusting the other.

But then Burbage winked at Septimus, and a message seemed to pass between the gray raven and his wily companion.

"Calm down, my dear old friend," Septimus said merrily. "Just give me your word that you'll keep this bag safe, and neither open it nor touch any of its contents until I return. We don't want another unpleasant accident, do we?"

"Very well. You have my word," said Pleshette, accepting the precious bag from Septimus.

After Pleshette closed the door on Septimus, he stowed the bag away, and paused to glare at the dozens of cages. "Who spoke?" he said.

The monkey pointed the gavel's handle at Paladin. "Not a word, not a whimper," he warned.

Pleshette stamped his foot. "Punch! Where are you? Who have you got up there? Must I bring back the gray raven? I will, you know. If you don't come clean with me, I'll clip your tail off and feed it to that mouse thief with salt, pepper, and ketchup!"

The monkey's eyebrows rose in fear. "Stupid, stupid, stupid," he murmured. Reluctantly, he unhooked Paladin's cage from the ceiling and swung down to the counter, dropping it roughly before Pleshette.

"Very good, my little rascal." Pleshette stroked the monkey's head and offered him a handful of bright red pistachio nuts. The monkey grabbed them eagerly and began cracking them open with his pointy teeth, then flicking the shells away.

Adjusting his glasses, Pleshette examined the cage.

"Oh," he said. "I've seen one of these before." He ran an ink-stained finger along the rivets and metalwork. "This is black magic, all right. Fine handiwork from Aviopolis. Steel fastenings. It's a melody lock, if I recall. An ingenious device that requires the trill of a robin to unlock it."

So that's the only way to get out of here, remarked Gabriel.

Pleshette scrutinized the raven. "Haven't we met before?" He shook the cage. But Paladin said nothing.

"Answer! Say your name, raven!"

When no reply came, Pleshette nodded to the monkey, who began hammering the cage as hard as he could. When this produced no result, the monkey flipped the gavel and poked it sharply into Paladin's wing.

"Stop it, please! I'm Paladin!"

The shopkeeper grabbed the monkey's gavel. A gleam appeared in his eye. "Ah, yes," he murmured. "So you *are* the Finley boy's bird. You'll be my insurance that Septimus won't make some private deal with that professor!" He placed the cage on a high shelf behind his counter and covered it with a sheet. "What a good day it's been. I'm in possession of a talking raven and a rune worth millions."

Just then the bell rang loudly, and Pleshette saw three children peering through the window.

"Go away!" he cried.

❋ The Breakout ❋

But the children would not leave. A girl with cat's-eye glasses and hair tightly braided in twelve short blond pigtails held up a shoe box for Pleshette to see. The boy beside her, a tall, gangly fellow with black-framed glasses, pressed the bell again. Another girl holding a violin case peered in hopefully.

Pleshette opened the door a crack. "Holy Harry Houdini, stop ringing my bell!" he snarled. "I don't want to buy cookies or whatever garbage you're selling."

"Hi there, Mr. Pleshette," said the girl with pigtails. "We found this talking raven, but never mind." She turned to her friends. "Let's go, guys!"

"Wait!" cried Pleshette, opening the door wide. "Another talking raven?"

He beckoned for the children to enter.

Pamela removed the lid to reveal Vyka. Pleshette peered at the marvelous blue bird from every angle and nodded. "Excellent condition," he said. "Where did you find it?"

"*Her,*" said Pamela, leaning her violin case against the counter. "She landed on my windowsill."

"And?"

"Asked me a riddle," said Pamela.

"*And?*" Pleshette's eyes widened.

"I couldn't guess it."

"Excellent! A raven without an amicus is even more valuable. I can certainly get a good price for it, and, of course, I would give you half of the normal share—"

"Wait," interrupted Pamela. "*Why only half?*"

"You're just children," said the shopkeeper. "You're half the size of an adult."

"But you're not buying *us.*"

Pleshette glared at them. "I have to pay taxes . . . foreign tariffs . . . fees, fines . . . surcharges!"

"No you don't," said Abby calmly. "You're making it up."

"But, my dear girl, listen to reason," continued Pleshette.

During this discussion, Somes had been looking around the shop for Paladin's cage. He couldn't see it among the items hanging from the ceiling, so he caught Abby's eye and shook his head.

"Maybe we should go," Abby said.

"All right, fine, no problem. You can have the normal share," said Pleshette hastily. "Let me hear her talk."

Pamela leaned toward Vyka. "Speak, little bird!"

The blue raven opened her beak and uttered a noise almost like a cork popping from a bottle: "*THROK! THROK!*"

Immediately, an answer came. *"THROK! THROK!"*

He is here, Vyka told Pamela, who signaled the good news to Abby and Somes.

"That's not talking," protested the shopkeeper. "You said she could talk."

"C'mon, little bird. Speak!" said Pamela.

Vyka uttered more throkking sounds.

All this time, Paladin and Gabriel had been listening carefully. *Gabriel?* said Paladin. *My friend Vyka just told me we're about to be released by your friends! You must be ready to jump free of me when the time comes. Do you understand?*

I'm ready, said Gabriel.

Pleshette was growing impatient. "You're not fooling me," he said. "This bird can't talk. Get out of my shop."

"No, honestly!" Pamela insisted. "I promise." She held up her violin case. "The raven loves music."

"Oh no." Pleshette clutched his bald head in despair. "A horrible screeching violin. I used to play one when I was a kid. It's the worst sound in the world."

Pamela opened the case, gently took out her violin, and started playing. A joyous melody filled the shop. Dozens of miserable captives peered out from their cages. Even Pleshette lowered his hands and listened, transfixed by the beautiful sound. His eyes settled on Pamela, as if he wished he could put her in a cage and sell her.

Meanwhile, Somes was eyeing a jar full of delicious-looking brown candies on the counter. Without glancing at the label, he reached inside, grabbed one, and popped it into his mouth. "Yum," he murmured. "Butterscotch!"

As he sucked on the candy, something strange began to happen: the room appeared to shimmer with a golden glow, and Pleshette's image suddenly split into two. The first Pleshette listened to the music, but the other looked annoyed, raised his hands in alarm, and shouted, "*Punch, get the cage!*" The lid of a large brass urn popped off and a small monkey with sharp teeth sprang out.

Puzzled, Somes watched the monkey jump onto the counter, swing above Pleshette, and remove a sheet concealing a raven-shaped cage. In another moment, the monkey had taken it through a back window and disappeared.

Somes turned to the urn. The lid was still fastened and there was no sign of a monkey. It was only then that he checked the candy jar label, which read CLAIRVOYANCE CANDIES, SEE THE FUTURE!

When Pamela lowered her violin, Pleshette sneered. "You play very well, but I think you're a liar," he said. "That raven hasn't said boo."

"Please, can I try one more time?" Pamela begged.

Pleshette shook his head. "Leave! All of you!"

"Just one more time," interrupted Somes, who tipped his head at the draped cage just over Pleshette's head. Then he rested his elbow on the lid of the monkey's brass urn.

Pamela played a trill of notes that sounded almost exactly

like the warble of a robin. She looked up at the shelf, hoping to see Paladin spring free.

"Punch, get the cage!" cried Pleshette.

It was exactly what he had shouted in Somes's premonition. A screech answered from inside the brass urn, but Somes kept his elbow firmly upon it.

"Try again!" Abby told Pamela.

Pamela played another trill. All eyes watched the shelf, but nothing happened.

"Punch, where are you?" demanded Pleshette.

The monkey shrieked from inside the urn. Somes held it shut.

"Again!" shouted Abby.

Pleshette grabbed Somes's arm. The lid flew open and the monkey scuttled out and scrambled across the counter.

A sharp musical trill cut through the air and the cloth fell from the cage as it snapped open.

Jump, Gabriel! cried Paladin, and Gabriel sprang clear of his friend.

Paladin saw the monkey reach for him, so he spread his wings and grabbed the monkey's tail with his beak. The monkey screeched and fought to escape.

Meanwhile, Gabriel had fallen on Pleshette. Before he could get his bearings, he felt himself being wrestled to the floor.

"Punch, I've got one of them!" yelled Pleshette.

But other hands grabbed Gabriel and wrenched him away. There were screams, shouts, and a door slamming. Footsteps pounded down a street. A monkey uttered a wail of pain.

"Come back!" shouted an angry voice.

Gabriel hobbled at first, stiff from his ordeal in the rigid cage, but Abby gripped his hand tightly and coaxed him to keep up with her. "Run, run, run! Just keep running!"

❋ Pleshette Sends Out Word ❋

"You should have known it was a trick!" Pleshette shouted at Punch.

"You shouldn't have let them in," countered the monkey, rearranging his tuft.

Pleshette's face turned crimson. "Tell me, my little rascal, how many other secrets have you kept from me aside from that raven cage? Do you think I'm stupid, stupid, stupid?"

The monkey cowered. "What about the runes?" he replied. "You still have them. And isn't Corax's rune worth millions? The valravens need to know you have their master for sale!"

The shopkeeper's greed swiftly replaced his rage. "Excellent, Punch." He drummed his fingers. "Now, how best to alert those moth-eaten ghouls?"

"Birds like to chatter," replied the monkey.

"Yes," said Pleshette with delight. "They certainly do."

*   *   *

As the sun descended over the rooftops, Leon Pleshette went for a stroll with Punch on his shoulder. He paused to light one of his disgusting Galimpong cigars. Noxious orange smoke began to billow around him; he coughed and spied a pair of starlings on the branch of a nearby maple tree.

"Punch, what a fine day it is!" he remarked in a loud voice.

"Why is that, master?" asked the monkey.

"Well, now that I possess the rune containing the Lord of Air and Darkness, the valravens have only to pay me my fee to gain their leader's freedom."

The starlings listened, horrified, but eager to hear every detail. After Pleshette had explained the fortune he expected to be paid for Corax's rune, the little birds took off to share the shocking news.

They told a party of finches gathered on a billboard, and the finches immediately told a grackle, who told a wren, who told a blue jay, who told some house sparrows, and that, of course, was like telling everybody.

The person most pleased to hear this news was, naturally, Corax, his soul still trapped inside the necklace around the robin's neck.

It grieves me that the boy escaped, he told Snitcher. *But we have no need of him now. The rune lies in Pleshette's shop, and my valravens will claim it soon enough. I have no doubt that Hookeye can raise any fortune needed to procure it, and bring me back to my former self!*

Snitcher called a meeting with Hookeye and the valravens on Cemetery Hill. Amid the solemn statues and mossy headstones, the phantoms converged. Puffing out his scarlet chest, the little robin hopped before a sea of sickly yellow eyes and tried to speak, but the ghouls jeered at him until Hookeye silenced them with a stern glare.

"Fellow valravens," intoned the one-eyed phantom, "His Eminence is trapped in a rune. We must raise a fortune to free him."

"Why not just steal it from the shopkeeper?" protested one valraven. "And drop it until it cracks open?"

Hookeye's mustard eye darkened. "Fool! The stone is delicate—one has been lost already. Would you dare risk the destruction of our *leader*? The shopkeeper must be paid."

The phantom pointed toward an immense marble bowl at his feet.

"Bring every jewel you possess, every trinket, every ring, necklace, and pendant. Every ruby, sapphire, emerald, and pearl!"

Hearing Hookeye's challenge, the valravens soared off to their hiding places and returned a few hours later with their valuables. One by one, each phantom hopped forward and plunked a few items into the bowl. Snitcher kept tally, describing each treasure to Corax.

By dawn, as the sky turned a bloody maroon, Corax sputtered with fury. *Tinsel? Bottle caps? Christmas ornaments? This is litter, clutter, scrap, and rubbish!*

The robin repeated Corax's thoughts to Hookeye, who

barked a challenge to his rancid followers. "We need *real* jewels. Who will find me diamonds and rubies?"

A confused silence followed this question.

"No one?" muttered Hookeye. "No one will help bring back the Lord of Air and Darkness?"

When no one replied, Snitcher uttered a valiant chirp, and hopped down to the bowl. He stared intensely at the junk, and suddenly, the torc started to glow. "I shall wish it, Eminence!"

There was a sudden burst of light. The bowl of trinkets began to glow, and soon it glittered with precious stones.

Hookeye chuckled. "Ah, here's what we need!"

But then the torc stopped glowing and the jewels darkened into dull lumps of coal.

Curse that blasted black magic, moaned Corax. *I should have expected some sort of trick. We must go about this the old-fashioned way—by theft and guile.*

Somewhere in the flock, a valraven spoke. "There's a spot I know," he said. "The finest jewels can be found there. Enough to pay His Eminence's ransom."

"Show me this place," ordered Hookeye.

At the Finley house on Fifth Street, Gabriel woke up in his own bed. It was Saturday. Paladin was perched on the bed knob with his eyelids shut, cooing softly in his sleep.

Gabriel recalled getting home the evening before and being welcomed with big hugs from his father and Aunt Jaz.

He stretched, wiggled his toes, and took a deep breath. "Mmm!" he sighed. His time in the stiff metal cage had made him appreciate simple things.

It was only after he dressed that Gabriel remembered what he had learned from his stay in Pleshette's shop. Septimus Geiger had found runes from Aviopolis, and one of them was likely to contain his mother!

This propelled him to talk to his father, but as he padded down the second set of stairs, he heard voices.

"Adam, old friend, I need to have an honest word with you."

Gabriel halted on the staircase. He recognized Septimus's voice, and remembered that the scavenger had promised Pleshette he would pay his father a visit.

"An *honest* word? Septimus, this is not like you," Adam said with a gentle laugh.

"My raven has heard rumors that Corax's spirit is commanding a very dangerous little robin who seeks his release. We must speak the truth to each other about these runes."

"*You* want to speak the truth?" Mr. Finley said skeptically. "Then I propose we drink a Flaming Truth Toddy—the elixir of honesty."

Septimus looked distressed. "But I thought the recipe was lost hundreds of years ago. At least, I hoped—"

"Well, my stove happens to make the tastiest one in town," said Adam.

"Must we?" said Septimus with reluctance. "Honesty is like red pepper—good for you only in small amounts."

The men stepped toward the stove. Adam kneeled down and whispered a request into the oven door.

Suddenly, there was a loud clank and the stove burst into action. Two mechanical arms began whipping up a concoction in a small copper pot until it glowed a brilliant blue. Then the arms poured this elixir into two glass tumblers and topped them with a flickering orange flame.

Adam and Septimus faced the stove, opening their mouths. The mechanical arms threw the toddies at them, and for a terrifying moment, Gabriel thought his father was going to burn to a crisp. Instead, however, they were bathed in a bright light for just a moment before a *SHAZZAP!*

The two men slumped contentedly into their chairs. "Delicious!" said Mr. Finley.

"The truth is tastier than I expected," conceded Septimus, patting down the smoke that curled around his coat. He looked curiously at Mr. Finley. "Be honest, Adam, what do you *really* think of me?"

"I think you're still as cunning as a fox and as slippery as an eel," Mr. Finley replied.

This satisfied Septimus that the drink was true to its name. "Well," he replied, "I think you're annoyingly well-intentioned and I hate your socks."

Adam raised his trouser hem and nodded. "I don't like them, either. Now, please, tell me about these runes."

"Oh, they're probably not worth much to anyone—"

Suddenly, blue smoke began to rise from Septimus's trousers. He sprang up. "Good heavens! What is happening?"

"You drank a Flaming Truth Toddy, Septimus," Adam reminded him. "Telling a lie sets your pants on fire."

Septimus hopped around the room fanning his trousers. "I mean that *one* rune may be *very valuable!*"

The smoke vanished, and Septimus sank cautiously back into his chair.

"Oh, Septimus," said Adam, laughing. "You and I both know that disappeared souls wind up in runes, and therefore Corax must be in one of them. I presume another rune contains your old friend, the raven Crawfin, and my dear wife, Tabitha, is in the third."

Septimus looked dismayed by Adam's swift guess, but then he seemed to realize his advantage. "Very good, Adam. . . . So we both have something to gain by working together. Help me free Corax and Crawfin and you can free your wife."

"No," Adam replied. "I want Tabitha back more than anything in the world, but I will not help you free my brother. Corax is a monster, and the world is better off without him."

"But think of the riches to be made!"

"How can you think of money, when his escape will bring war and bloodshed?"

Septimus frowned. "Aren't you forgetting that I know where your wife's rune is? You need my cooperation."

"I wish we could agree," said Adam. "But I wouldn't set Corax free for anything—even for the release of my beloved wife."

Septimus rose and paced the room, then glared at Adam. "Then we have nothing more to discuss."

Gabriel quickly retreated up the stairs.

After the front door slammed, he crept down again. He found his father sitting with his head in his hands. "Is there anything wrong, Dad?" he asked, not wanting to admit that he had been eavesdropping.

"Everything is wrong. But there's not much I can do about it."

"But there is, Dad," Gabriel replied. "I know where the runes are. They're in Pleshette's shop. I saw them."

Realizing that Gabriel had heard the conversation, Mr. Finley looked intrigued, but almost immediately, his smile faded. "I have just pledged on a Flaming Truth Toddy not to help Septimus. If I was to go to Pleshette's shop now, offering to help free Corax, I would burn up in a fireball."

"I don't get it," said Gabriel. "Does a pledge last forever?"

"No, no, the elixir wears off in about two or three days."

"But I don't have to wait," Gabriel declared. "I know where the runes are. What if I went and—"

"Absolutely not," interrupted Mr. Finley. "I almost lost

you just a day ago, Gabriel. Stay at home and be safe. That's all I ask. Two or three days isn't long to wait."

Gabriel nodded, although it seemed like an eternity to him.

"How can I just do nothing?" Gabriel asked his friends. "I know Pleshette has my mom's rune!"

They were on the stoop of the Finley house. Somes was copying a homework assignment from Abby's notes, while Abby enviously watched Pamela feed peanuts to Vyka.

"We should just go back and steal the bag of runes," said Pamela.

"Steal from Pleshette?" said Gabriel doubtfully.

"Technically," added Abby, "we'd be stealing something that had already been stolen, from a man who sells stolen things. In fact, it's almost a good deed, if you think about it."

"Yeah, really," Pamela said, and she offered the peanuts to Abby.

Nervously, Abby offered a peanut to Vyka. The raven was cautious but finally took it, then eagerly accepted more. Abby sighed with delight.

"Not so fast," said Somes. "How would we even get inside? It'll be years before he lets another kid in that store."

Vyka and I could get the keys out of Pleshette's pocket, Paladin said to Gabriel.

"Hey, Paladin has a good idea," said Gabriel, and repeated the raven's suggestion.

"So we all agree, right?" said Abby. "We're going to steal the runes?"

They all turned to Gabriel, who looked at Paladin.

The bird uttered a rallying *THROK!*

"Fine," said Gabriel. "Let's do it!"

❋ The Robbery ❋

A bald man buttoned his crumpled raincoat, locked his shop, and began walking. Without his green visor, his head resembled a big pink egg floating down Union Street.

Moments before Pleshette reached the Union Street subway station, however, he was intercepted by a black bird that swooped down in front of him, flapping its wings.

"Shoo," Pleshette snapped, waving his arms. "Shoo!"

Paladin mimicked his words. "Shoo! Shoo!"

"*Another* talking raven?" sneered Pleshette. "I've had enough of you! Shoo! Go away!"

He tried to drive the bird away, but Paladin hovered out of reach, and spoke again. "What do you call three toucans?"

"What? Three toucans? I have no idea!" said Pleshette.

"Answer a raven's riddle and you'll have a friend for life."

"Ah, yes," said Pleshette. He paused. "Fine. Let me see now. Three toucans . . ."

"A six-pack!" cried the raven. "Get it? A six-pack is three two-cans."

"Three two-cans? Oh, that's idiotic!"

Paladin circled the man, taunting him with more riddles. Soon Pleshette was so distracted that he didn't notice a second raven—one with unusual blue feathers—poking her head into his jacket pockets. After checking his left pocket, Vyka flew around to his right and, in a swift movement, withdrew a set of keys, then flew away.

Outside Pleshette's shop, Vyka flew down and dropped the keys into Gabriel's hand.

"Quickly!" said Abby.

Gabriel tested each key in the lock. The first two didn't fit, but the third slipped in perfectly and turned. Quietly, the children opened the door.

It was dark inside. Somes stretched a band of packing tape across the lid of Punch's urn. The occupants of the cages began to stir.

"You poor things!" whispered Pamela, looking up.

A chorus of cries, chirps, and squeals erupted.

"I'll free the snakes," said Somes.

"Wait, let me release the mice first," said Abby, "or the snakes will just have a feast!"

"I'll do the birds!" said Pamela.

They hauled clusters of cages down from the rafters. Somes unbolted the back door and the children began setting free every occupant—from crickets to mice, snakes, cockatoos, and parrots. Squeaks of relief erupted as the animals scampered, slithered, and flew away.

The biggest captive, a peacock-sized bird with iridescent gray feathers and strangely human eyes, regarded Pamela. "Felicitations for freeing us," she said. "Beware. The monkey is not in the urn." She raised her beak at the ceiling. "The monkey is *not* in the urn."

"Not in the urn?" repeated Pamela.

Gabriel had just emerged from the back, looking frustrated. "I found the leather bag," he said. "But there's nothing in it."

"Where could the runes be?" said Abby.

Just then, a shriek of laughter erupted from above and a hairy arm extended from a hammock swinging between the rafters. Delicate fingers produced a smooth gray rock. Punch's wicked little face appeared beside it.

"Stupid, stupid, stupid," sang the monkey. He tossed the rock into the air and caught it with his tail.

"It's a rune!" said Somes.

"Stop! Please stop!" cried Gabriel. "Whatever you do, don't let that fall!"

Punch giggled. "Stupid!" he hissed. "First you let all the animals out, and then you come to steal from me? Go home!"

The children were frozen in their footsteps, terrified of upsetting the monkey.

Punch idly tossed the rock in the air again, watching Gabriel's horrified reaction.

"Don't, Punch!" Gabriel shouted.

The monkey's tail caught it at the last moment.

"Stupid, stupid, stupid," whispered the monkey. "Nobody's smarter than Punch. Not one of you."

"You are a very clever monkey, that's true," said Gabriel in a soothing tone. "Smarter than Mr. Pleshette, I bet."

The monkey smiled faintly.

"But . . . ," Gabriel continued, "I bet you're not as smart as my friend Abby here."

The monkey looked at Abby doubtfully. "The one with no hair?"

Insulted, Abby put a hand to her head. That morning she had braided her frizzy blond hair into four tight pigtails, bound at the ends with the little glowing lights she'd worn at her birthday party. "I have plenty of hair," she replied. "And I bet I could answer any riddle you told me."

The monkey stared doubtfully at Abby's braids.

"No, really," persisted Abby. "I bet you one of those rocks."

"No way," Punch replied. "Not that stupid."

"How about if I lose, I give you a penny?" said Abby, digging into her pocket.

The monkey shook his head and grimaced, then pointed at Abby's pigtail with its glowing light. "I want that!"

"Too valuable," said Abby.

"Then no deal," said Punch.

Abby paused, tugging on a braid. "Okay, monkey," she said at last.

Pamela looked alarmed. "Abby, no."

But Punch swung from his hammock to a shelf, retrieved an enormous pair of scissors, and placed them on the counter. Then he sprang back to the ceiling and dangled a rune over the hammock with one foot while he recited.

"Neither solid nor air,
I float throughout the atmosphere.
The nearer that you get to me,
The harder that I am to see.
What am I?"

All eyes turned to Abby, who stared uneasily at the enormous pair of scissors.

"Neither solid . . . nor air, floating through the atmosphere." She took a deep breath. "Okay, well, that rules out a balloon or a zeppelin. The nearer you get to me, the harder to see. Oh, easy. It's a cloud, or water vapor—which is not solid, and not exactly air, either."

Looking annoyed, the monkey simply dropped the stone.

Abby lunged and caught it. "Got another one?" she said.

Punch took out another and turned it over in his slender little fingers.

"When the mountains crack like thunder
I escape my fiery source,
Swell across the fields and valleys.
If you touch me, I will scorch!"

"Another science riddle?" Abby sighed. "Science isn't my best subject."

The monkey seemed pleased to hear this. "Stupid, stupid, stupid," he whispered as he stared at her braids (perhaps wondering which one he would snip first).

"It's more like my second-best subject," she added. "No, wait, I'd say it was probably about the same as my favorite subject . . . which is riddles!"

Scowling, Punch spat into his free hand and resculpted the tuft of hair over his forehead.

"Anyway," Abby continued. "Mountains cracking open . . . sounds a bit like what happens when a volcano forms. What rolls down the slopes and valleys, and scorches? Molten lava scorches because it's red-hot, so that's my answer! *Lava!*"

A furious screech erupted from the hammock. Punch pelted the second rock at Abby. Somes caught it before it struck her.

"Okay, that's two. One more to go," whispered Gabriel.

Whimpering, Punch drew the third rock from the hammock, tossed it into the air, then caught it with his tail. Narrowing his eyes to a hostile squint, he recited the final riddle:

"This pair is in the briny sea,
In every meal (except for tea).
Safe to eat they'll always be,
But not when taken separately."

Abby shot a worried glance at the others. "I know what this is. But I don't know the answer!"

"How can you know, but not know?" said Pamela.

"Because," began Abby, "this pair is in the briny sea. Briny means salty, okay? Salt is in almost every meal except for teatime, because nobody puts salt in a dessert. Safe to eat they'll always be. Well, salt is safe to eat, but the answer is a pair."

"Salt and pepper?" said Gabriel.

"But that can't be right," said Pamela. "You can eat pepper or salt separately. The riddle says these two things are not safe to eat separately."

The monkey spun the stone up and caught it in his mouth, spit it out, and caught it again with his tail.

Somes turned to Abby. "When I was in the hospital my dad's doctor told him to cut down on sodium chloride— that's salt, isn't it?"

"Somes!" Abby threw her arms around him. "You're a genius! Sodium and chlorine, that's the answer. Separately, one explodes and the other is a poison, but together they make salt!"

"Abby, look out!" cried Gabriel.

The monkey had climbed down, seized the scissors, and sliced off the topmost braid on Abby's scalp.

"*You* were supposed to answer it, not him, stupid!" cried the monkey, waving the braid over his head with treacherous glee. He unraveled the little glowing light from Abby's braid, threw her pigtail to the floor, and fixed the light to his own tuft.

Abby touched the bare spot on her head, and her look of triumph melted into shock.

Meanwhile, Gabriel and Somes lunged at the monkey, but Punch flung the stone up in the air with his tail.

"I've got it!" cried Gabriel, leaping after it.

"I've got it!" said Somes, jumping higher.

The boys' heads struck together while the rock spun in an elusive arc, falling past their fingers to the floor—where it shattered into pieces.

"No!" cried Gabriel.

❋ Only Two ❋

"**W**ell," sighed Mr. Finley, "I've got good news and bad news."

Gabriel, Abby, Pamela, and Somes stood in his study with worried faces. Mr. Finley had been scrutinizing each of the two remaining stones. Finally, he lowered his magnifying glass and dusted off his hands.

"I'm very impressed," he said. "You solved the monkey's riddles. If not for your amazing wits and bravery, I would be yelling at the four of you for being so foolish, careless, and oblivious to your own safety."

"I'm sorry, Dad," said Gabriel. "But when I heard what Septimus said to you this morning, I had to do something."

"And going to Pleshette's shop was my idea, Mr. Finley," said Pamela. "You can blame me for that, and I'm sorry."

"And I'm really sorry for suggesting we steal the runes," added Abby as she probed the bare patch on her scalp where the monkey had cut off her pigtail.

Mr. Finley turned to Somes, the only one who hadn't apologized.

"Well . . . sorry, but I'm *not* sorry," Somes said. "We set all those creatures free. That was a good deed . . . and the monkey, well, Abby kicked his butt with each riddle. The only thing I'm sorry for is . . . if that rock had Gabriel's mom inside."

"Please, Mr. Finley?" said Abby. "Tell us she wasn't in it."

"No need to be sorry, Somes," he said, raising an eyebrow at the boy. "I believe Septimus left Pleshette with a bagful of duds. Common rocks, probably."

"But one of them was real—the dwarf who exploded—I saw that happen," said Gabriel.

"I'm sure Septimus intended to steal them all, but perhaps he had a difficult time removing that first one and gave up on the others," said Mr. Finley. "So he gathered some rocks, hoping to bluff Pleshette into buying them. Pleshette probably promised him a fortune for Corax's rune, much more than he dreamed."

"Wait a minute," said Gabriel. "The stork told us that the captives had to be freed with a riddle."

"A riddle, right!" said Pamela. "*That's* the thing I forgot to tell you, Mr. Finley."

Mr. Finley looked pleased. "This should have been obvious to me," he said. "It takes a riddle to free a rune. And Septimus despises riddles. You can be sure that he'll want me and my riddle-solving expertise along when he returns to the Chamber of Runes. The only problem that remains is this Corax business."

Gabriel regarded his father curiously. "Dad, when the elixir wears off, couldn't you just agree to help free Corax, but free Mom instead?"

Mr. Finley was silent for a moment. "Gabriel," he said, "I promise I will do everything possible to free your mother. But I will not risk freeing my diabolical brother. As you know, Corax's valravens wiped out whole species of birds and dominated and enslaved thousands of creatures in Aviopolis. If he was set free, I could be responsible for the misery and despair of millions of people, too."

They were all quiet after this. Even Gabriel, desperate as he was, didn't know what to say.

"On the other hand," Mr. Finley added, "you may be sure that Corax's valravens will find a way to pay for his release, and Septimus will come back to me for help."

"And what will you do?" asked Gabriel.

Mr. Finley heaved a long sigh. "I shall have to think of some clever solution."

As they walked with Somes back to his house that evening, Gabriel and his friends tried to imagine how the valravens could come up with enough money to pay for Corax's freedom. Would they pay by cash, check, credit?

"They might rip wristwatches from Wall Streeters," said Somes.

"Pinch coins from parking meters," chimed Pamela.

"Swipe diamonds from engagement rings," said Abby.

"Wring gold bling from hip-hop kings!" quipped Gabriel.

"Steal some paintings from a fancy museum."

"Then charge lots of people a fortune to see 'em!"

"Find the world's biggest oyster on Rockaway Beach."

"And pull out a pearl as big as a peach!"

After they had stopped laughing, Pamela wondered aloud if the valravens might simply give up.

"You'd better hope they don't, for Gabriel's sake," said Somes.

"Why?"

"Because his dad needs to find his mom's rune, and Septimus knows the way."

"This is so twisted," said Pamela. "So the only way Mr. Finley can free Gabriel's mother is to help Septimus free Corax, too?"

"Yeah," said Gabriel. "But it's more than twisted. It's a catastrophe."

A week passed. Gabriel still hadn't seen any valravens; and though he kept an eye out for Snitcher on his windowsill, the bird did not appear.

Pamela knocked on his door on Wednesday evening, after everybody else had gone to bed. "Gabriel," she said, "don't you think it's strange that you can get Paladin to sleep in your room, but Vyka won't set foot inside mine?"

"Oh," Gabriel replied, "I think it's because I found Paladin when he was just a chick. But Vyka is a wild raven. She's cautious with people and scared of being caged."

"Then why isn't she afraid of me? And why did I become a raven's amicus when Abby is so much better at riddles?"

Gabriel shrugged. "Who knows?"

"And why can I get the stove to cook, when you, Abby, and Somes can't?" Pamela continued. "And why was I the only one who could get the writing desk to cooperate? That is, until it ran away from me."

"I don't get it, either." Gabriel paused thoughtfully. "But I bet somebody in this house has the answer."

Pamela reacted with a start. "Gabriel, it has to be my mom!"

"You're kidding," he replied. "She doesn't believe in magic at all."

Jumping up, Pamela said goodnight and left his room. A moment later, Gabriel heard her playing the violin, a bold, purposeful tune that seemed to hint she was concocting some plan to get the truth out of her mother.

The next morning, Trudy Baskin and Pamela boarded the subway and sat down. They watched the car fill up with passengers at the next couple of stations. Then, when it was crammed as tight as a sardine tin, the train began its long underground trip toward Manhattan.

It was at this moment that Pamela turned decisively to her mother. "Mom, who is my dad, really?"

Trudy fidgeted in her seat. "You're asking me here? Now?" she said.

"I want to know."

"I told you, dear." Trudy lowered her voice. "His name was Ramsey Baskin."

"Was that his real name?"

"It was the name . . . he gave."

"Whatever that means," said Pamela. "Did you love him?"

"Love him? Of course. I always loved him."

Pamela's eyes narrowed slightly. "When did you meet him?"

Trudy blinked nervously. A nun with a trembling chin peered up from her newspaper, eager to hear Trudy's reply.

Trudy glared at the nun, whose face swiftly disappeared behind the newspaper. She looked at Pamela. "This is a *terrible* time to ask these questions! I will not say another word."

Pamela waited about a minute, then turned to her mother again. "I know, Mother. I know what the truth is. I just think it's time you admitted it, that's all." This was a big gamble, because Pamela, of course, had nothing but a hunch.

She continued to wait, eyes locked on her mother's.

Trudy was thunderstruck. How could Pamela *possibly* know the truth? she wondered. She had been keeping this a secret for such a very long time. It was embedded in her—

almost a part of her body. She feared she might actually fall to pieces if she revealed it now.

She fanned herself and let out a deep sigh, and then she realized that all eyes in the subway car had settled on her. Their intensity was unnerving. Passengers craned their necks in expectation. Then a woman in a leopard-skin pillbox hat gave her a smile. A man with a goatee wearing a vest and an alligator tie clip murmured a soft noise of sympathy. A pair of girls sharing a picture book gave Trudy a nod, as if to say "Go ahead! Tell your daughter what she wants to know." Even the nun dipped her quivering chin in encouragement.

Trudy took a deep breath. "When I was a little girl, I liked Jasmine's older brother, Corax," she began.

"I know," said Pamela—because she really did know this.

"And he ran away from home."

"Right."

"But sometimes he returned very briefly to see me. He would appear on a crowded street and pass me a note that said something sweet like 'I've been thinking of you.' Sometimes he asked me for news of his family. It was his way of keeping in touch. He was ashamed, you see, but too proud to go back home.

"Those visits were always extremely quick, and months . . . or years . . . apart. Until one day he appeared at my door," Trudy continued. "By now he was all grown up. He told me he'd been studying ancient mythology and rare objects and collecting peculiar pieces of art. He was ashamed of the person he had been as a boy, he explained. Something sad had happened back then, a terrible event that had made him run away. So he'd made a fresh start and changed his name to Ramsey Baskin. I promised to keep his past a secret."

Trudy paused, and a sweet expression filled her eyes. "You see, I knew that I'd loved him for a long time. We were so happy together that we married. And that was when you were born, my dear."

Pamela's mouth fell open.

Around her, the subway passengers looked enthralled. The train came to a halt, and a group of them reluctantly got off—the nun and the man with the alligator tie clip were especially hesitant to leave. Only the girls remained.

"But there's more, isn't there?" Pamela asked.

Trudy nodded. "The night you were born, a snowstorm buried the whole city. The ambulance couldn't get to me, and I had to call Jasmine to help because I was going into labor. I remember that I glanced out the window and there were ravens everywhere. Their bright yellow eyes watched me from the trees, fences, and lampposts."

Pamela shivered. "Ravens don't have yellow eyes, Mom."

Trudy paused. "Why, yes, they do, dear."

"I think what you saw were valravens."

"*Valravens?* Well, whatever they were, I hated them."

Trudy paused for a moment.

"There was another baby," she said at last. "You see, I was carrying twins."

"What?" cried Pamela. *"Twins?"*

"Jasmine arrived and helped deliver you, and she tucked you into the crib, and then I gave birth to your brother. He was a strange little thing, hardly looked like a baby at all. I remember his terrified little eyes. He was so small and frail, like a little bird. . . ."

"A bird?"

The train stopped at the next station. The two girls were led reluctantly away by their mother.

Now that she had revealed this much, Trudy couldn't stop. She talked faster. "He looked like a bird because . . . he was so small and delicate, I mean. Such big eyes. I was terribly tired after his birth, and I fell asleep while Jasmine cleaned him and wrapped him warmly."

"So I have a brother," murmured Pamela.

"But later, when I woke, I saw a horrible sight. A huge raven stood before me, with black feathers, big wings, and eyes like yellow beacons, and he was holding my baby boy, and I fainted."

Trudy blinked and clutched Pamela's hand. "I never saw my husband or my little boy again." She paused, turning a ring on her finger. "That raven must have taken them away."

Trudy drew in a deep breath and looked at Pamela with tears in her eyes. "I knew it made no sense; I was afraid people would say I imagined things and think I was mad. It was better to say that it never happened. Jasmine promised she would take care of us. 'Family is family,' she said, and she's always kept her word."

Pamela didn't speak for a moment. Had Corax transformed into a valraven before her mother's eyes and terrified her? Had he taken the baby—her brother—away? Why? Her mother's memory seemed so confused, and yet there was sense in what she said. She still loved this mysterious man, and Pamela was his daughter, Mr. Finley's niece, and Gabriel's cousin.

Now she understood why she could paravolate and how she had inherited the Finleys' ease with mojo-mechanisms. But the final fact, the one that horrified her, took a while to sink in.

Pamela repeated it a few times to herself, just to believe it.

My father is Corax Finley, the Lord of Air and Darkness.

❈ Attack of the Valravens ❈

"**A**h, Pamela, come in," said Aunt Jaz. She was correcting homework that afternoon, curled up in a large wicker arm-chair in her bedroom.

The air felt so clear in this room, perhaps because it was filled with plants, vines, and a large rubber tree with shiny oval leaves reaching to the ceiling. The collection of objects on Jasmine's mantelpiece offered a hint of her curiosity and knowledge about unusual things—a gyroscope, a lemur's skull, a trilobite fossil, and a mermaid's purse.

"Aunt Jaz?" Pamela began cautiously, settling her eyes upon the marching animal figures on the carpet at her aunt's feet. "I know Corax is my father. Today I found out from my mom that she had twins the night I was born, and that she couldn't remember what happened after that. She said I have a brother."

Pamela expected Aunt Jaz to be surprised, but her voice was calm and sensible. "Yes," she said softly. "I was waiting for you to learn the truth, my dear. After all, you're entitled to it. Perhaps I can elaborate on the details, as I'm sure your mother was in a state when she told you." Aunt Jaz patted a wicker ottoman and plumped its cushion. "Come sit, and I'll explain."

When Pamela was settled, her aunt began. "On the night of your birth, Corax, your father—the Lord of Air and Darkness, if you will—had an awful choice to make. He thought he could give up the life of a merciless overlord when he married your mother, but when she gave birth to you and your brother, he had to choose between two paths."

"Because my brother was a valraven?"

Aunt Jaz looked startled for the first time. "Your mother told you this?"

"No," admitted Pamela. "I guessed that part. If my father is a valraven, then he might have had a son who was at least *part* valraven."

Aunt Jaz nodded. "Yes, I'm afraid so. And a newborn valraven must eat flesh within minutes of being born or he will perish. Corax couldn't let him die, so he chose to leave Trudy and you and raise the boy somewhere safe."

"Where?"

"Aviopolis, of course."

"But didn't he have to feed him first?"

Suddenly, Pamela remembered the scene she'd witnessed in the snow globe with her friends. "Somes's father was attacked on the night of a blizzard by a creature that bit off the tip of his finger! Could that have been my father, feeding my brother?"

"Why, yes. Fascinating," agreed Jasmine. "You know, I

thought the baby didn't survive that night, but if what you say is true, then he may be alive today—somewhere."

This gave Pamela a curious new feeling of hope. "I wonder if my brother knows that I exist."

"My dear, I think it is unlikely. There is no reason I can imagine that would have caused Corax to tell him about you, I'm afraid.

"What a night that was for your poor mother," Aunt Jaz continued. "She saw Corax in his valraven form and it terrified her. She has been scared of ravens ever since. She was so tormented by nightmares for the next few days that I decided to help her. I used the stove downstairs to make a potion that clouded her memory."

"So she doesn't know what really happened?"

Jasmine sighed. "Pamela, her memory was merely obscured to ease her pain. It was not erased. She may one day choose to remember the truth—that Corax is a valraven who carried away his valraven son—but that is entirely up to her."

"She told me that she was afraid people would think she was crazy."

"My dear, half the world worries that people think they're crazy."

"And the other half?"

Aunt Jaz shrugged. "The other half *is* crazy."

Pamela smiled in spite of herself as she wiped away a tear. "So I have a brother I've never met, and a horrible monster of a father who doesn't ever want to see me or care if I exist."

Aunt Jaz put her arm around Pamela. "My dear, if a person calls himself Lord of Air and Darkness and condemns thousands of creatures to serve him or die, he creates many enemies. Perhaps he has done you a kindness."

As the Finley house went to sleep that night, Pamela lay in bed, puzzled, excited, and horrified. *My father is Corax! Lord of Air and Darkness. He ate the flesh of his amicus and became a hideous half man, half raven. He wiped out dozens of species of talking birds and ruled Aviopolis in the cavernous depths beneath Brooklyn. His hunger for the torc's magic was so fiendish that he locked his own brother—Adam Finley—in a dark cell for years, and almost killed Gabriel.* She trembled as a horrible realization occurred to her. *Corax spoke to me in Aviopolis when we rescued Mr. Finley just months ago. He invited me and my friends to join him in his quest to conquer the world without knowing I was his daughter.*

Pamela shuddered at this memory, and yet she was proud to have stood up to the demon at the time.

But she felt different about her brother. *Maybe he's a valraven,* she thought. *But he must be part human, too. I wonder if we're anything alike. He's never known our mother. I've never known our father. There's so much we could tell each other, and so much to learn!*

Her thoughts wouldn't settle, so after tossing in bed for an hour, Pamela threw on her robe and padded downstairs.

The stove suddenly stirred into activity and offered her a cup of steamy hot chocolate. Pamela took a few sips, then wandered into the backyard and listened to the whispers of the tall oaks swaying above her.

Vyka? she thought, hoping the raven might be near. *Are you there?*

And then it occurred to her that Vyka might be disgusted by her. *What if she can read my mind and knows that I'm Corax's daughter?* she worried.

Vyka? she thought. *Please, Vyka, answer me!*

I'm here, came a reply.

Oh, please don't be afraid of me, said Pamela, detecting the raven's cautious tone. *I would never do anything to harm you, I promise!*

What if Corax were to command you?

I'd rather die. You can hear my thoughts, so you must know that I would never betray you.

Nor would I betray you. But you must be prepared for those who will question our loyalty. When ravens or humans learn that you are Corax's daughter, some will suspect us of being his servants. Are you ready for that, Pamela?

I am.

The moment Pamela said this, there was a swift movement behind her. The blue raven alighted upon her shoulder. *Oh, please, Vyka,* Pamela said. *Let's paravolate right now, the way Gabriel and Paladin do.*

I can't wait! said Vyka, laughing with relief.

The girl and the raven faced each other, concentrating as deeply as they could.

Raising her arms, Pamela let her fingertips quiver for a moment; then she jumped. A strange ripple spread through her body, extending to the tips of her fingers and toes.

The experience of merging is never quite the same for any two people. Pamela didn't feel crushed and crammed inside Vyka's body (as Abby had in Hookeye's). It felt more as if she'd slid entirely out of her own skin and into Vyka's with the ease of slipping into a snug, warm bed. Pamela felt her bones adjust, her shoulders roll backward, her legs shorten, her toes extend into talons, and her skin become alive with thousands of feathers.

The transformation ended with a jolt.

In that instant, they took to the air. The rooftops of Brooklyn spun away beneath them. Sirens, honks, and the noisy roar of the city softened and became as faint as the rustle of leaves on a blustery fall day.

It was like coasting on an endless wave. Pamela rose and dipped, sometimes with immense speed, sometimes as gently as a feather before a faint breath. Great swells of air lifted her high, then cast her off into smaller, more vigorous streams. Now she understood the joy of the lark and the giddy delight of a flock of seagulls. Flying was bliss.

The sky, however, was not a quiet place that evening.

As they flew higher, a tumult of furious air currents wailed and howled around them. Yet there was almost nothing to see but the star-filled sky. Presently, a vast cumulus cloud drifted toward them, hundreds of feet high, layered with soft peaks and fluffy canyons. The shrill wind quieted, leaving a damp, majestic silence. Then the great cloud passed, the whistling winds and moaning breezes resumed, and the raven dropped altitude in search of a more peaceful area of sky.

Below them, the city lights glowed in a soft, sleepy haze. Pamela saw a lonely ferryboat chug its way across the bay. They veered toward Manhattan and flew over glittering clusters of skyscrapers and the tiny headlights of cars weaving down streets in orderly processions.

But the quiet was interrupted by sirens wailing on Fifty-Seventh Street. Vyka swooped down to see what the commotion was about. She landed on a large clock marked with the name TIFFANY & CO.

Outside this famous jewelry store, police cars skidded to a halt, their bright lights flashing. Yellow tape reading CAUTION was stretched across the sidewalk. Police officers tried to restrain a crowd of curious onlookers while reporters swarmed the store's entrance.

An important-looking man with white hair stepped out from a cluster of detectives. He dabbed his forehead with a handkerchief as a boisterous crowd of reporters surrounded him.

"Any information on who stole the diamonds from Tiffany's, Commissioner?" one reporter asked.

"As a matter of—"

"Is it true that the doors sprang open *as if by magic*, Commissioner?"

The commissioner tried again. "In fact, it—"

Another reporter shouted, "What about suspects?"

Furious, the commissioner raised his hands for silence. "For buttered bagel's sake, will you please let me talk? This robbery was conducted by . . . ahem . . . birds."

"Birds?" laughed a reporter. "Puh-leeze!"

The commissioner turned red, and looked for his deputy chief. "Inspector Ramirez, will you explain?"

A short woman wearing a gold badge stepped forward. "That's right, sir. Birds were seen leaving with diamond jewelry dangling from their mouths—er, I mean, beaks. The perps were birds."

"That's the craziest thing I've ever heard," said yet another reporter. "Do you have any evidence?"

"*Plenty,*" said the commissioner. "All the security cameras show them."

"Seriously? What kind of birds?"

"Ravens!" barked the commissioner, and he hurried into the building.

At that very moment a reporter looked up and noticed Vyka. "Hey, there's one now. Maybe it's come back for seconds!"

"Arrest it, Officer!" joked another.

Inspector Ramirez called for her officers to steer the reporters back behind the barricades.

"C'mon, Officer," said a third reporter, laughing. "Time to start rounding up witnesses. Start with *that* bird!"

Immediately, Vyka took to the air, and soon she and Pamela were soaring high above the city again.

Vyka, would ravens really steal diamonds? asked Pamela.

Absolutely not, the raven replied. *My cousins, the jackdaws and crows, love glittering objects, but none of* them *are thieves. I'll bet they were valravens.*

Of course! said Pamela. *I have to tell Gabriel right away.*

A swift air current bore them across the East River toward home. Fog circled the Finley house that morning as Pamela sprang free in the backyard. She invited Vyka to come inside, but the raven reminded her that she was wild, and preferred to see the sky above her. *I will always be near,* she told Pamela as she spread her wings and took off.

Pamela waved goodbye, entered the house, and dashed upstairs to Gabriel's room. "Wake up!" she whispered, shaking him. "I have something amazing to tell you!"

"What? What happened?" he murmured.

"Well, first of all, I'm Corax's daughter! We're *cousins*, Gabriel. My mother married him when she was younger, and had twins. Corax took my brother away because he looked like a valraven."

Confused, Gabriel rubbed the sleep from his eyes. "You're Corax's daughter? You have a brother who's a valraven? *What?*"

Next, Pamela explained about the memory elixir that

Aunt Jaz had given her mother. "Corax left with my brother before my mom understood what he was. Aunt Jaz thinks she could remember the truth if she wanted to."

Gabriel sighed. "So Aunt Jaz has known all this for years? Y'know, it's ridiculous how many secrets there are in this family."

"Oh, Gabriel, all families have secrets," Pamela replied.

"I guess," he admitted. "How does it feel? I mean—to have a valraven brother?"

Pamela looked uneasy. "Aunt Jaz didn't think he survived, until I told her what we saw in the snow globe. I wonder where he is now."

"Aviopolis, I bet."

"Poor guy," said Pamela. "I mean, to grow up in a world without sky. Without light. I wish he knew about me."

"Maybe he does."

"Gabriel . . ." She hesitated. "Do you think he could be evil?"

"*You're* not evil," Gabriel replied quickly.

Pamela went quiet after this. What was his name? she wondered. Did he look human, or was he a cursed, shabby-feathered ghoul like the valravens she had seen in Aviopolis?

At that moment, Gabriel's alarm clock rang.

"Oh," said Pamela as he switched it off, "there's a part I forgot to tell you. I flew with Vyka for the first time, and saw the police and a huge diamond robbery. We think it was done by valravens."

Gabriel sat up when he heard this. "Diamonds!" he said. "The perfect way to pay for Corax's rune."

"Which means they'll go to Pleshette to try to buy it. The only problem is that Pleshette doesn't have any runes. . . ."

At that moment, Paladin arrived at the windowsill. *Guess what!* he said, hopping excitedly up and down. *The sparrows say there's been an enormous diamond—*

"Robbery?" said Gabriel. "Yeah, we know." He quickly explained that Pamela and Vyka had paravolated to the scene of the crime.

"Paladin, why were you out so early this morning, anyway?" Gabriel asked.

I wanted to spread the news that Pleshette's runes were fake, said Paladin.

After Gabriel told Pamela this, she grew excited. "I guess now Septimus will be scurrying off to get the rune from the Chamber of Runes so that he can exchange it for the diamonds."

Gabriel sprang to his feet. "I have to tell my dad!"

❋ The Flaming Truth ❋

Taking the steps three at a time, Gabriel caught up with his father on the way to breakfast and told him about the robbery.

Mr. Finley scratched his beard thoughtfully. "So the valravens are ready to pay. I must call Septimus—"

He stopped talking as footsteps came down the stairs.

It was Aunt Jaz. She had arranged her hair differently this morning. Auburn ringlets framed her face, and she wore a turquoise necklace and a beautiful deep-green silk dress.

Mr. Finley was surprised. "Jasmine, you're all dressed up," he said. "Are you going to a funeral?"

Jasmine's smile vanished. "No, Adam. As a matter of fact, I'm going out tonight."

"Oh, beachcombing? Skull collecting?"

"I happen to be going on a *date*. Is that so hard to imagine?"

"A date?" said Mr. Finley. "Have I met this person?"

"No, you have not."

"I think you look awesome, Aunt Jaz," interjected Gabriel.

"Thank you, my dear," his aunt replied. "A *funeral*. Really!"

Mr. Finley fled into his study, followed by Gabriel. He was about to dial a number on his phone when he noticed his son watching him from the doorway.

"What's up?"

"Hey, Dad," Gabriel began. "If Septimus needs you to go with him to the Chamber of Runes, can I go, too? What I mean is, I want to help you bring Mom back. I know it's dangerous—"

Mr. Finley interrupted him. "Better get some breakfast, Gabriel."

"You might need help."

"You'll be late for school if you don't eat now," his father replied, and gestured for him to close the door on his way out.

While he ate his cereal, Gabriel told Pamela that he thought his father was going to see Septimus. Big things were surely about to happen.

"Don't go *anywhere* without me!" Pamela whispered as she scrambled off to school.

Mr. Finley showed no sign of being aware of his son's concern when he entered the kitchen. He calmly poured his coffee and munched on his toast. Gabriel stole furtive glances at his father, accidentally spilling milk over the rim of his bowl. As Mr. Finley looked down at the newspaper, Gabriel sensed that he wasn't reading it.

Gabriel threw on his coat and fussed with his shoelaces. It took five minutes to tie them, a record. Finally, he turned to his dad. "I think I'm getting sick."

"No fever," replied Mr. Finley, feeling Gabriel's forehead. "If it gets worse, tell the nurse and she'll call me. Better hurry, you're going to be late."

Gabriel nodded and trudged up to the front door, dragging his backpack. He noticed Paladin preening his feathers on the banister. "I thought you were still upstairs, asleep," he said.

How could I sleep with all that's going on? replied Paladin.

Gabriel glanced downstairs and decided to speak telepathically. *Paladin, could you keep an eye on my dad? I'm afraid he and Septimus are going to Aviopolis without telling me.*

Of course.

This assurance was the only thing that propelled Gabriel out of the house.

He found Somes and Abby waiting for him at his gate. As they hurried to school, he shared the news about Corax, Pamela's brother, and the jewel theft.

"So Corax attacked my dad to get flesh to feed his baby valraven?" Somes said. "*That's* why my dad has been so messed up all these years? A tiny bite from the tip of his pinkie finger? Who knew a valraven bite could drive a person crazy."

"Your dad isn't crazy, Somes," said Gabriel. "He's friendly to us—sometimes."

"Trust me, you can be crazy *and* friendly," Somes replied. "Not to mention mean, angry, nasty, and horrible, especially to your own kid."

As they walked downhill, Somes strode ahead of his friends. He kicked a trash can, then thumped a garden gate. At the next intersection, he struck the pole with his fist, then winced with pain.

Abby spoke softly to him. "Aren't you glad to know what happened, at least?"

Somes nursed his fist. "I guess. And he's been better these days, but . . ." He stopped talking as his eyes welled with tears. He removed his glasses and wiped his eyes with his sleeve.

The three friends stood quietly for a moment. Somes blew his nose and glanced wearily at Gabriel and Abby. "I'm okay now," he whispered. "Thanks, you guys."

Somes knew that he could count on them not to laugh or make fun of him.

"I hope I never run into that valraven kid," Somes said. "For all the stuff I've been through, I'd have to teach him a lesson."

By now, they had reached school. Gabriel felt another

pang of anxiety as he thought about his father. Even the statue of Alfred Grimes, one eye concealed by a patch, seemed to regard him with foreboding.

At the top of the steps, Gabriel noticed Aunt Jaz chatting with Mr. Coffin. He paused, and heard a chorus of gravelly squawks from above. A large flock of black birds was flying in close formation over the trees. Were they ravens or val-ravens? he wondered.

During math class, Mr. Coffin walked behind Gabriel and stopped.

"You're very unfocused, Mr. Finley. Something wrong at home?"

"No, Mr. Coffin."

"You've drawn a man with a beak and wings on your worksheet."

Gabriel was startled to see that he'd drawn Corax in the margin.

Mr. Coffin examined the sketch more closely. "Who is that?"

"Nobody," Gabriel answered quickly.

"He looks like a nightmare," said Mr. Coffin, picking up the paper. "One has to conquer one's nightmares, or they haunt you for the rest of your life."

Gabriel stared at Mr. Coffin. Then he saw a tattoo on his teacher's wrist that he'd never noticed before.

It was a raven in flight—a silhouette, no bigger than a penny.

Paladin was true to his word: he perched in the hall, watching Adam through the doorway of the study. When the doorbell rang shortly after lunchtime, a tall gentleman with snow-white hair, a tweed suit, and a snappy silk scarf greeted Adam at the front door.

"Septimus Geiger at your service!" he said.

The raven hopped down the banister rail so that he could hear their conversation.

The stove swiftly produced a bubbling potion in a copper pot. Moments later, there was a loud *SHAZZAP* as Mr. Finley and Septimus Geiger were bathed in a flash of light.

"Delicious!" Septimus issued a loud burp and patted the smoke from his shirt and trousers as he sat down. "Well, Adam, that was a fine toddy indeed. And I'm glad you've changed your mind. So you'll free Corax?"

"I didn't say that, Septimus," Mr. Finley cautioned him. "Remember, we can speak only the truth here, and I know the runes you left with Pleshette were duds, so tell me where the real ones are."

"If I must, I must," Septimus muttered, wiping his forehead nervously with a handkerchief. "There's another entrance to Aviopolis in Coney Island. It leads to the Chamber of Runes through a maze somewhere on the eastern rim of the great cavern. There, the runes sit on a pedestal surrounded by blue fire. I could only get one off the pedestal. There are three left."

"Ah, so you *did* try to sell fake runes to Pleshette?"

Septimus shrugged. "That was Burbage's idea." He looked cautiously at his pant legs, but they didn't smoke. "*Definitely* Burbage's idea," he added. "Pleshette's very angry with me, not to mention upset with your son for freeing his animals. That boy has a fine talent for thievery. I could get him started on a wonderful career."

"As a thief?" Adam looked furious. "Absolutely not!"

"Suit yourself." Septimus looked indignant, as if this were the most generous offer in the world. "But that reminds me of a riddle. How do you turn a thief into a chef? Can you guess?"

Adam paused for a moment. "I haven't a clue," he said.

"Like this," said Septimus. "Take his eye, steal his tea, and start him off at sea."

"What? That makes no sense at all," replied Mr. Finley.

Septimus raised an eyebrow. "I hope you're not losing your touch, Adam. The answer is simple. If you take 'i' and 't' from the word *thief* and begin it with 'c,' you've got *chef*."

Adam raised an eyebrow. "Did *you* solve that riddle when you first heard it, Septimus?"

"No, I couldn't solve a riddle to save my life."

Adam sat up straight, as if he had just had an inspiration. "Look, old friend," he said. "I have bad news for you."

"What?" Septimus glanced at his trousers in case they were on fire again.

"You cannot free Corax from his rune without answering a riddle. So if you wish to let this monster back into the world, you will have to sharpen up your riddling skills."

Septimus's snowy-white head sank between his shoulders. "More blasted riddles," he groaned. "It's not fair. All those diamonds, just waiting for me!" Then he glanced cunningly at Adam. "I remember your wife's rune. Such a pretty little silhouette. Imagine her, waiting all these years to be rescued. Poor lady. Seems a pity that you'll never find her."

Mr. Finley didn't reply.

Septimus leaned closer. "Adam, consider my offer: answer the riddle for Corax's rune, and then free your wife and live happily ever after."

Mr. Finley gave a dramatic shrug. "You've made your point, Septimus. I'll go with you."

Septimus looked startled. "Really?"

"Yes."

"And you'll answer the riddle to free Corax *before* you try to free your wife?"

"I shall," said Adam.

"Promise?"

"If I were lying, my pants would be on fire," Adam replied.

Septimus scrutinized Adam's trousers with surprise. "Very true. Then we'd better hurry. I have a suspicion that Pleshette is going to try to beat me to it."

"But how would he find his way there?"

"Burbage," muttered Septimus. "Pleshette bribed him with a cageful of mice."

As the two men threw on their coats, Paladin quickly retreated upstairs to Gabriel's room. The window had been left ajar, just in case he needed to slip outside.

Little did the two men know that a robin had also been eavesdropping on their conversation from the kitchen windowsill. His beady black eyes darted back and forth from Septimus Geiger to Adam Finley, until their last words confirmed what he wanted to hear. Now he began hopping up and down like a windup toy, gleeful and triumphant.

"Your Eminence," he chirruped, "they're going to the Chamber of Runes!"

I can hardly believe it is true, replied the voice in the robin's head. *It surprises me that my brother, Adam, would free me, and I am even more doubtful that Septimus Geiger has the courage to do it. We must warn the valravens not to release a single diamond until my spirit and body are reunited.*

"What is the first thing you'll do, Eminence?" asked the robin.

I shall crush those who betrayed me, and take back my domain. My dear son, Cassius, must be wondering what has happened to me in the month gone by. When I find him, we shall begin our conquest of the sunlit world.

❄ Journey to the Chamber of Runes ❄

As soon as the afternoon bell rang, students began to stream out the doors of the Alfred Grimes Academy like minnows escaping a sturgeon—none of them as fast as Gabriel, Abby, and Somes. When the light turned green at the intersection, they darted across the street, past the deli, the sneaker shop, and the pet-grooming parlor, turned left on Fifth Street, and sprinted past brownstones and shady oaks toward the Finley house.

"What did Paladin say?" asked Abby, when Gabriel mentioned that the raven had alerted him telepathically.

"He said that my dad had left with Septimus for Aviopolis," said Gabriel.

"What are we going to do?" Somes replied.

Gabriel stopped to catch his breath before answering. "Follow them, of course. My dad and Septimus are heading to Coney Island on the subway. Paladin is going to find out where they go once they get off the train."

"Wait, Paladin is following them? But the train goes underground."

"Yeah." Gabriel began running again. "Haven't you ever seen pigeons hop a ride on the train?"

"Well, sure," admitted Somes. "But I thought they were lost."

As they crossed Sixth Avenue and hurried up the last block, Somes thought of more questions, but he was too breathless to ask them. In front of Gabriel's house, they found Pamela and Vyka waiting on the stoop. Gabriel quickly explained what he knew.

"So we'll follow your dad, even though he said not to?" Pamela replied excitedly.

Gabriel paused to think. "That's the weird thing. He didn't tell me not to follow. He just told me to go to school."

The friends passed several hours in the Finleys' kitchen as shadows from the afternoon sun stretched across the floor. Every few minutes, someone asked Gabriel if he had heard from Paladin. "Telepathy doesn't work like a phone," he finally explained. "I never know if he hears my questions. We just have to wait."

Eventually, Abby dashed over to her house and returned lugging a bulky backpack. She was about to explain what she had brought when Gabriel raised his hand. "Shush!" he cried. "Paladin's talking to me."

The train has stopped and Mr. Finley has stepped out with Septimus

Geiger. We're in a big building with open doorways. I hear seagulls. I smell the sea and hear waves crashing upon sand. In the distance, I see a big white frame of crisscrossed logs with a carriage that rides up steeply and drops down terrifyingly fast—it's some sort of human torture device.

"That's the old Cyclone roller coaster in Coney Island," said Gabriel. *We're coming, Paladin,* he replied.

Abby unfolded a subway map and traced a line toward the sea. "Stillwell Avenue station, the last stop," she said.

Pamela stepped into the yard to talk to Vyka. *Will you come with us on the train?*

I'd rather fly, replied Vyka. *I'll meet Paladin at the end of the subway line.*

The blue raven took off and vanished beyond the rooftops.

The foursome scrambled out of the house and headed in the direction of the subway station. They had only reached the corner when they recognized a figure coming toward them.

"That's Mr. Coffin!" said Abby.

The math teacher was carrying a bouquet of fiery tulips. "Hello," he said, nodding.

"Mr. Coffin," said Gabriel, "this is my friend Pamela."

"Pamela, yes, I've heard of you," he said. "I was just on my way to your house."

"You've *heard* of her? *My* house?" asked Gabriel.

Mr. Coffin held up the flowers. "Your aunt and I are having dinner tonight."

"Oh," said Gabriel. "OH!" It suddenly occurred to him that Mr. Coffin was the mysterious friend Aunt Jaz was meeting for her date.

Mr. Coffin noticed Abby's full backpack. "Hello, Ms. Chastain. Are you going on a trip?"

"No, no," said Abby, trying to sound casual. "Nowhere, really."

Mr. Coffin regarded her with an amused stare. "Well, it's none of my business," he said, digging into his coat pocket. "But this might come in handy." He held out a big round hook with a wooden handle. "Here, take it, Somes."

Somes turned the odd device in his hand.

"Have a good trip," murmured Mr. Coffin as he continued on his way.

"Weird," said Somes, examining the hook. "He always seems to know more than he says."

It was six miles from the Finley house to Coney Island as the crow flies, and a prevailing wind rushed Vyka across Brooklyn in less than ten minutes. When she glanced back the way she had come, the sky was darkening, as if a storm—or something infinitely worse—was approaching. For a brief moment, she glimpsed a flock of black birds, but they disappeared in the dense clouds. Pamela had warned Vyka to look out for valravens, so she was startled when a black bird swooped alongside her.

"Greetings, Vyka!" Paladin cried.

Vyka answered with her silvery laugh, recognizing him. "Greetings, Paladin! Have you found Mr. Finley?"

The two ravens flew down and perched together on a streetlamp.

"Over there," said Paladin, tipping his head toward the corner of Mermaid Avenue. Two men were having a conversation. The first was bearded and wore a corduroy jacket. The other was tall and gangly, with snow-white hair and a silk scarf.

The birds flew down and cautiously circled the men, eager to hear their conversation.

"There's one thing I don't understand, Septimus," said Adam Finley. "How did you find this way into Aviopolis? It's miles from the old one."

"Oysters," replied Septimus with a cunning smile. "Burbage and I came for some fried oysters one day when I noticed the road being repaired. There was a great dark hole, and suddenly a flock of shabby valravens flew down from the sky and into it."

"What induced you to go exploring underground?" said Adam. "I thought you hated the dark."

"I certainly do," said Septimus. "But Burbage reminded me that if we found a way back into Aviopolis, we might find jewels. You see, if carpenters scatter sawdust where they work, and bakers leave flour, it stands to reason that the crafty fellows who built Aviopolis out of jade, quartz, gold, and rubies would leave jewels on the floor."

"And did you find any?"

"No, but we found the Chamber of Runes." Septimus stopped, and nodded to the left. "Quick, turn down this street."

Paladin and Vyka were following the men from a distance, eager to report back to Gabriel. But a jeering voice broke their concentration. "Here's a riddle for you! What begins with 'r' and ends with 'n,' is black as night, and can't fly?"

"A dead raven!" answered another voice.

A grim cackle followed this unpleasant answer. Paladin looked behind him and saw two valravens.

"Greetings, friend of Finley!" cried one, extending his talons.

Paladin changed direction, performing a backward loop that completely confused the two valravens, who collided in a cascade of feathers.

"Vyka, watch out!" cried Paladin.

Above him, he saw two other valravens grab the blue raven by her wings. Paladin soared toward them and struck the first bird with the point of his beak. The stunned phantom uttered a gasp and rolled through the air in an awkward tumble.

Vyka fought her way free of the other bird's grip. "Thank you," she said.

"Listen!" Paladin cried. "There are more!"

The coarse jeers of other valravens filled the air.

"Traitors!"

"Enemies!"

"Betrayers!"

"Renegades!"

The shrill voice of a robin broke through the taunts. "Capture them or kill them! I don't care which!"

Paladin recognized the rim of silver around the robin's neck. "Beware of him, Vyka. He's the one who—"

"Paladin, look out!" interrupted Vyka.

Struck from behind, Paladin felt a searing pain as sharp talons grabbed him by his metacarpal bones.

In a flash, Vyka pierced the attacker with her beak, but another valraven swooped down with claws extended. Vyka twisted to elude it and tumbled out of sight.

Paladin fell free and flapped his wings to gain speed.

"Vyka! Vyka!" he cried, looking around. "Where are you?"

And then something else occurred to him: he had lost Adam Finley and the entrance to Aviopolis.

❊ Tillie ❊

When the foursome stepped out of Stillwell Avenue station, they were confused.

"I thought you said Paladin and Vyka would show us the way," said Somes.

"We were supposed to meet right here," said Gabriel, looking around. "Maybe they're still following my dad."

"I hope nothing's wrong," said Pamela.

In the distance, they heard the croaky calls of ravens. Sooty clouds filled the sky, and the air felt prickly and charged. They started walking toward the sound of the birds.

The streets of Coney Island were empty, yet there were hints of the summer season to come. The brightly painted gondola rides and spinning platforms in Luna Park stood stark and still against the sky. An empty wooden promenade extended over a level beach, while seagulls coasted playfully on waves as they crashed to shore.

A faded mural of a fun-house face was painted on a building near the boardwalk—his broad, insane grin gawked at the children as if to say "I know why you're here!"

"What a horrible face," said Pamela, shuddering.

"It's called Tillie," said Gabriel. "There are tons of versions of him, but this mural is the biggest one I've ever seen. It must be pretty old; the paint is peeling."

"What a joker," said Somes. "He's laughing at us for coming all the way out here without a clue."

Abby polished her lenses and walked up to examine the mural. "Hey, look at his teeth." Her voice rose with excitement. Tillie's smile had a row of teeth as big as tombstones. "There are words painted on them. They're very light, but . . . Can you guys see?"

They all gathered around and began reading the words, one by one.

"Welcome . . . ," read Somes.

"Stranger," continued Abby.

"Welcome . . . ," said Pamela.

Gabriel shook his head impatiently. "This is taking too long. Everybody, just call out your words quickly, and we'll figure it out together."

Trying again, they barked out words one after another so that it sounded like this:

Welcome, stranger; welcome, friend.
You have reached your journey's end.

From this spot your purpose lies
Way beneath these sunny skies.

Banished far from light and air
Lies a demon in despair,
Ringed by flames of azure fire,
Punished by his own desire.

If you dare proceed from here,
Gird your courage; veil your fear,
Overlook the sand and mortar,
Seek an entrance beneath water.

Gabriel swallowed nervously. "'A demon in despair.' That sounds like Corax."

"'Far from light and air'—that sounds a lot like Aviopolis," added Pamela.

Somes, however, was staring at the gray waves breaking on the shore. "'An entrance beneath water.' How are we supposed to find it without drowning?"

"'From this spot your purpose lies,'" read Abby. "Look, I don't think we need to move from 'this spot.'"

"But there's no water right here, Abby," said Gabriel.

Abby pointed down. "Don't you see it?"

Beneath her sneakers was a manhole cover with the word WATER on it.

"Oh, *water*. I get it." Somes grinned.

He kneeled down and tried to lift the iron cover. "No handles," he grunted.

Gabriel noticed several finger-sized holes. "If only we had something to poke into this . . ."

"A *hook*!" Somes held up the device that Mr. Coffin had given him. "How did he know?"

They didn't waste time discussing it. Somes wriggled the hook into a hole and, with a deep grunt, slid the manhole cover aside.

A set of rungs went down the wall of the manhole. The children climbed in and followed the rungs down, down, down underground.

There was almost no light.

Abby reached into her backpack and produced four sets of little flashlights set on headbands. "I had these from summer camp," she explained. "My uncle gave me the set so my tentmates and I could get to the outdoor toilets without stepping on a porcupine in the middle of the night."

"I hate outdoor critters," said Somes, strapping on his headlamp.

They walked single file along a brick-walled tunnel, feet sloshing through a thin layer of fetid water as their lights scanned the wet and slimy walls. After several minutes, they arrived at a rough-hewn opening in the brick. Cool air blew from the dark hole and a new smell filled their nostrils—not of brackish water or rot, but something much worse. It was the odor they remembered from their last visit to Aviopolis.

The odor of ghastly things that never saw the sun—silent, hungry, suffocating things.

Abby hesitated. "Keep going?"

"I think so," said Gabriel.

"Yeah," said Somes.

"Yep," added Pamela.

Two things kept their feet moving forward. First, they were together. Second, Gabriel's father was somewhere ahead.

Before them lay a narrower passageway that dipped down at a steep angle. The tunnel proceeded for about one hundred feet, then veered sharply left and plunged downward again. Their footsteps became louder and clumsier as the path before them grew steeper.

"Please, guys," said Pamela. "Not so fast!"

"I can't help it," said Somes. "I feel like I'm being pulled forward."

As Gabriel gripped the damp rock walls to slow himself down, small things slithered through his fingers. He hastily pulled his hands away.

"It's like one of those paths inside the pyramids," whispered Abby.

"You've been in a pyramid?" said Somes skeptically.

"I read that the tomb is always at the bottom of a steep passageway."

"You're freaking me out," said Somes. "I hate pyramids,

tombs, and mummification. The ancient Egyptians scooped out peoples' brains and put them in jars."

"Only if you were a pharaoh," Abby said.

Gabriel came to a sudden halt; the others bumped into each other and uttered urgent hushes.

The sudden quiet was terrifying. It felt like a *thing* trying to creep into their ears, blocking all normal sounds. If you've ever hidden in a coat closet, you might know this sound— just your heart pounding, squishing blood through arteries and veins. A silence with nothing to corrupt it but the noisy mechanical racket of your own body.

Somes couldn't bear it; he struck his foot hard against the ground, just so he could hear something. There was an echo, and when he raised his hand, he felt a cold breeze above his head. He looked up and saw a cavern extending above him for hundreds of feet.

When the four friends started walking again, they realized they were in a sunken channel with steep, rocky sides. Occasionally, they peered through a crack in the surface and saw an immense shadowy landscape beyond.

"Somes, stop that!" said Abby.

"What?" replied Somes. "What am I doing?"

"You're making a sound with your feet."

"Am not."

The slithering sound grew louder and, quite suddenly, the breeze above them ceased.

Somes reached up and felt a smooth ceiling instead of open air. "Weird," he said, for he could still see the cavern beyond the ceiling, although it was blurry.

The ceiling moved, scattering pebbles upon everybody's shoulders. This was followed by another slithering sound, then silence.

Gabriel felt an impulse to play dead. He couldn't explain it; he just knew that to lie still was the wisest thing. "Lights out. Everyone down," he murmured. "On the ground, quick as you can. Don't make any noise."

❈ The Power Station ❈

Paladin finally spotted a blue streak dodging several val-ravens. Vyka weaved skillfully between trees, then dipped under the roof of an outdoor elevated subway station. The ravens chased her, careering into people on the platform. One raven burst right through a man's open newspaper.

Vyka flew toward a gray substation surrounded by barbed wire and shiny cone-shaped objects. She perched on an electrical wire next to a sign reading DANGER HIGH VOLTAGE. A deep, ominous hum hinted that millions of volts of electricity were traveling through the wires leading into and out of this dull gray building.

Hookeye circled the substation while Snitcher fluttered impatiently behind him. "What are you scared of? Go get her!"

"Shush! This power is almost as strong as the torc," said Hookeye. "Hear that hum? Its flash will cook us to a crisp."

"But His Eminence commands you to get her," said Snitcher.

"Silence, little one," snapped the one-eyed valraven.

Paladin circled the substation, spooked by the dreadful hum. He hovered near the blue raven. "Vyka, you were very brave, but shouldn't we get out of here?" he cried.

"As long as we don't touch the ground, the wires are safe," Vyka assured him.

Paladin alighted beside her on the wire and felt relieved when nothing happened.

"See?" she said. "You just have to know where—"

She was interrupted by another voice.

"Not just where, but when and how many watts!"

"Many who trespass on owl territory make a *shocking* mistake and get a *revolting charge!*"

"What kind of charge? Assault and *battery?*" quipped a third, coughing hysterically.

"Oh boy," murmured Paladin. "I've never heard so many stupid puns in my life. We must be among owls."

"Owls?" said Vyka with alarm. "They're as dangerous as valravens."

Four great horned owls settled on a wire above the ravens.

"I know these guys," Paladin told Vyka. "Greetings!" he said to the predators. "I'm Paladin and this is Vyka. Is my old friend Caruso here?"

"Not *currently,*" quipped an owl.

"He's feeling a bit *dim* in the *bulbs!*" said another.

"I think he's had a *power failure!*"

"Perhaps he'll feel more *positive* in the morning!"

The owls coughed with amusement at their electrical jokes.

"Greetings, Paladin, protector of the torc and friend of Gabriel Finley," said the first owl when he had calmed down. "Where is your amicus?"

Paladin explained that Gabriel was on his way, hoping to follow his father to the Chamber of Runes. When he mentioned that Septimus wished to free Corax, the owls became very upsct.

"Corax will be impossible to defeat if this happens. The robin will serve him and the torc will be his to control," worried one.

"But surely the Finley boy should be able to summon the torc with the ash-wood staff," said another.

"Oh, the staff," said Paladin. "Gabriel left it behind when we chased the robin out of Aviopolis."

"In that case," said the first owl, "we'll do all we can to help you."

An owl's guarantee is a fine thing. Their claws are strong, their beaks as sharp as daggers. Although they had refused to reveal the location of the Chamber of Runes in the zoo, they were eager to help now. So Paladin and Vyka felt very safe as they were escorted to the location of the manhole cover.

Paladin scratched at the letters reading WATER and peered anxiously through the holes. "This is too heavy for any of us to lift," he said.

"A *grate* disappointment," chortled one owl.

"I felt *sewer* we could lift it," quipped another. But this joke just drew groans from the other owls.

Gabriel? Can you hear me? said Paladin, trying telepathy. *Are you there?*

The raven turned anxiously to Vyka. "I feel that he's down there, but he won't answer me."

Vyka agreed. "I know Pamela's there, too."

"How can we help them if we can't even enter?" Paladin asked the owls.

"You may be more helpful above than below," advised one owl. "The sparrows gossip that great hordes of valravens are coming with a trove of diamonds in anticipation of their leader's release."

❋ Denizen of the Darkness ❋

With their headlamps switched off, the friends lay on the ground, hearts pounding. The monstrous presence above them suddenly shifted, and more dust fell upon their shoulders.

Somes couldn't stay still any longer—he snapped on his headlamp and looked up. A milky glass ceiling reflected the light's beam. Transparent riblike shapes caught the light, and floating objects passed by, suspended in what appeared to be a clear jelly.

Suddenly, the whole ceiling shifted, and Somes realized what it was.

When he told Abby, she went rigid. "Oh, gosh, gosh, gosh," she muttered.

"What?" said Pamela.

"It's a megamorphic see-through *thing*," said Somes.

"A what? And how can it be see-through?" asked Gabriel.

"I forget what they're called," said Somes.

"Haven't you seen those pictures of living things in the deepest trenches of the ocean?" whispered Abby. "They don't need color because nothing can see them, so they're transparent. No pigment at all."

"Will it eat us?" asked Pamela.

"I don't know, but I can see what it's *eaten*." Somes's hand trembled as he pointed the beam at things floating in the clear ooze: a milk crate, a soda bottle, boots, and a winged skeleton.

"If we just stay still, we'll be safe. Right, Abby?" asked Somes.

"Unless it's a snake," Abby replied.

"Why?" asked Gabriel.

"Most predators can't see you if you keep still. But snakes have thermal vision; if you're warm, you glow like a red light. Our only chance is to be cold and dead."

"I think it's a snake," said Somes miserably. "It looks like a snake."

"I have a snake," Abby announced. "His name's Mr. Squirmington. And he only eats live food. But you can spook him pretty easily."

"So how do we spook a snake that's a zillion times bigger than we are?" wondered Gabriel.

Somes looked at Pamela. "Did you bring your violin?"

"Not this time," she replied.

"Snakes can't really hear the way we do," Abby reminded him. "All that stuff about snake charmers hypnotizing cobras with music is horse poop. We need another way to scare it."

"I don't want to be bitten," said Somes. "Not by teeth as big as ninja swords."

"Don't worry," said Abby. "We'll probably be swallowed whole, then dissolved by acids in its stomach. It'll take months."

Suddenly, Gabriel noticed a pain in his belly; he wasn't sure if it was fear or simply hunger, but it seemed a bitter fate to be digested while feeling hungry, too. "Hey, Abby," he said. "What do you have to eat in your backpack?"

"Snack bars left over from last summer," she said.

Gabriel rummaged through the backpack. "What's in these boxes?"

"Boxes? . . . Oh, sparklers from the Fourth of July. Last year it rained all week, so I never used them."

"Do you have matches?" said Somes.

"Of course," said Abby.

"A box of flaming sparklers might freak out a snake," said Gabriel.

Abby passed the sparklers around and then lit them. As sparks began to fly, the serpent quivered and shifted with obvious distress.

"Wave them around!" said Gabriel.

Exaggerating their gestures, the children made brilliant shapes in the darkness.

The creature's reaction was swift. Startled and confused, it drew its body into tight coils, its glassy ribs contracted, and its thin, transparent scales quivered. Prominent fangs were visible behind a weaving tongue, glossy and clear as glass.

Abby was quick to point out that snakes can swallow something three times the size of their own heads. "Even if you hid inside a small car, this thing could swallow it."

"Oh, great. Thanks," muttered Somes. He lit more sparklers and tossed them at the snake's eyes.

This startled the serpent more than anything else. It reared up and hissed.

"Everybody!" cried Somes to the others. "Copy me!"

The others threw their sparklers at the snake's head. One of Pamela's struck it in the eye. It immediately jerked away from them.

"Good one, Pamela!" cried Gabriel.

As the serpent retreated in frantic movements, its enormous limpid body rustled across the rocky surface, coils winding a graceful and swift escape into the darker recesses of the cave.

"We did it!" shouted Abby. "Now let's just hope we don't bump into it around another corner."

Giddy at having defeated the serpent, the foursome hurried along the tunnel. Occasionally, they caught a glimpse of a vast abandoned city above them. Their headlamps moved too quickly to illuminate much, but Gabriel saw fallen pillars and fragments of pediments and archways. He counted hundreds of windows—all dark and vacant: the remnants of Aviopolis.

Everyone began to complain of being hungry, so they finished off the snack bars from Abby's backpack.

Presently, they came to a fork in the tunnel. The little group hesitated.

"Let's split up," suggested Gabriel at last. "If one of us gets somewhere, we'll call out."

"Okay," said Somes. "C'mon, Pamela," and he took the right turn.

Gabriel and Abby headed left.

"Wait, Somes!" cried Abby, moments later. "We're at another fork."

"We found a fork, too," called Pamela. "Let's meet up and figure this out."

"Tunnels going in every direction with no signs," said Abby when they'd joined up again. "This must be a maze."

"No, no, it must lead somewhere," said Pamela.

"Look what I found," said Somes. He held up a dirty, round object. As their headlamp beams converged, they recognized the eye cavities and teeth of a human skull.

"Ugh." Somes dropped the skull and wiped his hands on his pants. "I hate this place."

Abby rubbed her glasses. "Why would anyone build a maze here, anyway?"

"To make the Chamber of Runes hard to find?" suggested Gabriel.

"Or," said Pamela, "so we could die of thirst or hunger before we find it."

A grim sense of despair settled over the group.

"Wait a minute," said Gabriel. "Does anybody remember Mr. Coffin's riddle? He put a maze on the board and said even a blind person could find the way out."

"That was a just game," Somes said. "*This* is real."

"Yeah, but the rules are the same," said Abby. "Follow the wall and it will lead you out. It's the rule."

"Unless there are a bunch of exits. Then we'll still be lost," said Somes.

"Okay, guys, we can give up and go home," said Pamela. "Or we can give it a try. What do you think, Gabriel?"

Gabriel looked at their faces. He didn't want any of his friends to come to harm. On the other hand, he felt so close to finding his mother and was convinced that his father would need his help in some way. "Let's do it," he said.

"Remember, Septimus got through the maze," said Abby with a hopeful smile. "And he's a chickenhearted scaredy pants."

"Follow the wall," said Gabriel, looking at the others. "Okay?"

Everybody nodded. Gabriel took the first left fork, touching the tunnel wall lightly with his left hand. The corridor split, then split again, as onward they walked. There were many dead ends, but they always stuck to the wall on the left, no matter how it turned and twisted. They moved quickly as they became comfortable with the plan, and the speed of their pace made them more confident.

"Gabriel?" whispered Abby after a while. "Don't you think it's weird that Mr. Coffin has helped us twice on this trip?"

"And I'm still wondering about that raven tattoo on his wrist," said Gabriel. "And the thing he said about fighting your demons. I wonder if he was talking about Corax."

"Hey, don't be so sure he's a good dude," muttered Somes from behind. "He gave me two Ds and marked me down for missing Friday's homework."

A half hour later, the twisting corridor of rock opened upon a plateau with a gloomy view of ruins extending across the floor of a vast cavern. Just ahead, a gleaming passageway of smooth, shiny blue stone seemed to beckon to the children. As they ventured forward, the air became warmer and the corridor reflected light from some distant source. The foursome shed their jackets and headlamps in a heap and continued toward the beckoning glow.

Abby paused and squinted at the passage wall. "It's lapis lazuli," she said. "A kind of gemstone."

"How do you know that?" said Somes.

"My sister Etta makes earrings out of it."

"Of course she does," said Somes, rolling his eyes.

"There's nothing wrong with knowing things," Abby added.

Pamela gave Somes a warning glance. When he said nothing, she pinched him.

"Ow!" he cried. "Why'd you do that?"

"That wasn't nice," she said.

Gabriel stopped and turned around. "Guys? Chill, okay?"

The polished blue corridor curved around to a point where they couldn't see its beginning or end, but then they heard a familiar voice. "The remarkable thing about the language of Gutnish is that there are twenty-six words for darkness."

It was Adam Finley. He spoke in a pedantic tone, as if lecturing to a hall of students.

Septimus's voice replied, "You don't say."

"There's *goyt*, which means the darkness of a gold mine," Adam continued. "*Doyt*, the darkness of a tomb; *hoyt*, the hopeful darkness before the dawn; *poyt*, the pitiful darkness of being alone; and *boyt*, the wholesome darkness of strong Gutnish beer. There's also—"

"*Goyt, doyt, hoyt, poyt, boyt!*" interrupted Septimus. "Get to the point!"

The children tiptoed toward the voices and came to two open brass doors. Beyond the doorway, Mr. Finley and Septimus Geiger could be seen in a domed room. The ceiling curved down to the floor, and in the room's center stood a round pedestal rimmed by lapping blue flames. Several stones rested within the circle of fire.

Adam and Septimus peered at the stones. Each one appeared to be translucent, with a silhouette in its center.

"Those *must* be the real runes," whispered Gabriel.

Septimus turned around. "What are you doing here?" he snapped. "Finley, you promised you were coming alone."

"I *did* come alone," replied Adam.

"Sorry, Dad," said Gabriel. "I had to."

"We almost got eaten by a big glass serpent," interrupted Abby cheerfully.

"Serpent? Oh, you mean the subterranean rock boa," said Septimus.

"It's okay, we scared it away," said Pamela.

"With sparklers," added Somes.

"Oh, I wish you hadn't," said Septimus.

"Why not?"

Septimus scowled. "She keeps the valravens away."

"We haven't seen any valravens," said Gabriel.

"The subterranean rock boa eats them," explained Septimus. "Of course, if she disappears for a few days because of your stupidity, the valravens will be back, screaming for fresh meat."

"She could have eaten *us*," said Gabriel.

"Nonsense! She's as pleasant as a pussycat." Septimus sniffed. "Whales are huge, but they don't eat people, do they? It's such arrogance to think you're worthy of being eaten."

Gabriel looked over at his father, expecting him to be upset. But his father seemed pleased that he had arrived.

"Look here, Gabriel," he said. Mr. Finley pointed to one

of the three runes. Inside, Gabriel saw a small silhouette of a woman. Just a shadow, but her head turned, suddenly, as if she'd noticed him. Gabriel felt a sudden ache in his chest.

"It's her," said Adam. "Your mother."

Gabriel reached toward the stone, but Septimus grabbed his hand and jerked it away.

"Let's be clear on one thing," he said sharply. "Your father promised he'd free *Corax* first. That was his oath, sworn on a Flaming Truth Toddy."

"Really, Dad?" said Gabriel with disbelief.

Mr. Finley looked apologetic. "It was the only way, Gabriel."

"Can't you change your mind?"

"No, he can't!" Septimus barked. "If you break a promise made with a toddy, your pants will burn like a bonfire." Septimus put a tender hand to his scorched trousers. "Take my word for it."

Mr. Finley tried to reassure Gabriel. "Everything will be fine. I must do exactly what I promised. I must try to free Corax," he whispered softly. "But at least now you know where your mother is. . . ."

As his father's voice trailed off, Gabriel realized that Mr. Finley had been counting on Gabriel to follow him all along. And this made him wonder why his father had agreed to such a terrible bargain.

❋ The First Mistake ❋

"**N**ow we get to the hard part," said Septimus.

Three runes glowed in the circle of fire. One contained the silhouette of a woman, one the silhouette of a raven, and one a creature, half man, half valraven.

Gabriel looked up at the letters of an unfamiliar language shimmering on the ceiling of the domed chamber.

"This is Gutnish," Mr. Finley explained. "I was just saying that the dwarfs—"

"Had twenty different words for a toothache," murmured Septimus.

Mr. Finley gave Septimus a withering glance. "That the dwarfs built this chamber, the torc, and the whole city of Aviopolis, and they left instructions for the release of its captives." He pointed to the markings above his head. "If you stare long enough, the scribbles will change into a language you understand. The walls read your mind and translate themselves." He read the first two verses:

"Here you find three silent prisoners
Held in magic's cold suspension.
Some are saintly, some are evil.
Not one came by his intention.

"The runes contain three souls preserved—
A pure one by misfortune served,
A raven by his friend, disserved,
A devilish one by greed interred."

"'A pure one.' That's Mom, right?" said Gabriel.

"Yes, disappeared, but through no fault of her own," said Adam Finley.

"And 'a raven by his friend, disserved'?" whispered Abby.

"Alas, poor Crawfin, I knew him well," Septimus said with a sigh. "Disserved by me. When I wore the torc, I wished he would disappear and . . . here he is."

Septimus dabbed an eye with his handkerchief.

"The 'devilish one by greed interred' must be Corax—my . . . um . . . dad," said Pamela.

"Right, because when I dueled him, he wished for all the torc's power, but the torc absorbed him instead," said Gabriel.

"So what will happen when his body escapes the rune?" asked Abby.

"He will be pleasantly gratified," predicted Septimus. "He'll congratulate us and order his valravens to pay me a fortune in diamonds!"

"Do you actually believe that?" Mr. Finley replied. "Once Corax's spirit and body are reunited, he will seize the torc and wreak revenge on all of us, and the world above."

"Oh, cheer up, Adam. It won't be that bad," said Septimus.

"Mr. Finley, where are the riddles that have to be answered?" asked Abby.

Gabriel's father pointed up at the shimmering letters, which had transformed into another verse:

Reach into this fiery circle
For the soul you dare release;
Only with the riddle's answer
Will its grip upon you cease.

If you err in your solution,
Surrender to a wretched state—
Eternity inside this chamber
With the souls who share your fate.

Now Pamela asked the question they were all wondering. "Mr. Finley, what if you fail?"

"As the words say, I shall become captive in this chamber. But I have absolute confidence that Gabriel will do the right thing and walk out of here." Mr. Finley gave Gabriel a long, intense stare. "Is that clear?"

Gabriel looked anguished. "Just walk out? Mom's been

stuck inside a rune for twelve years. And if you get the riddle wrong, you become a prisoner, too?"

"That's the way it works. You see, the ancient dwarfs who built Aviopolis loved riddles," explained Mr. Finley. "A king banished them underground—so, for one hundred years, they shared riddles to pass the time. It was just a game to them, like bowling or chess—"

"Riddles all day? For one hundred years? I would have gone bonkers," muttered Septimus.

"Actually," said Adam, "there are five words in Gutnish for being driven bonkers by riddles. One of them is—"

"Please, may we proceed?" said Septimus with a sigh.

Mr. Finley gave Gabriel a tight embrace. "I know you'll do the right thing," he repeated. Then he rolled up his sleeves. "Well, I'd better get on with it."

"Dad, please, don't help Corax—" Gabriel began.

"He has no choice," interrupted Septimus. "He promised."

Mr. Finley put his hands through the circle of flames. The fire did not burn him, but when he clasped the rune, his body went rigid. "I—I can't move my arms or legs," he said.

On the stone ceiling, letters appeared. They made no sense at first, but as Gabriel stared, they slowly changed into familiar words:

What gets shorter as time grows longer?

"Let me see. . . ." Adam took a long breath as he thought. Beads of sweat began to roll down his cheeks. He offered a brief smile to Gabriel, then turned back to the rune and said, in a loud voice, "The answer is *trees!*"

"No!" protested Abby. "A *candle* gets shorter as time grows longer. Why did he say something that gets *longer?*"

There was a tremendous earsplitting roar in the room, and Adam vanished.

"Dad!" cried Gabriel.

A fourth stone appeared in the ring of fire. Horrified, Gabriel kneeled down and peered at a faint silhouette of a bearded man within the translucent stone.

"Dad! Can you hear me?" said Gabriel. "Please, Dad?"

The figure seemed oblivious to Gabriel's voice.

"Oh, my God," said Pamela.

"So much for promises," said Septimus bitterly.

"And . . . such an easy question," murmured Abby with disbelief.

It was then, however, that Gabriel realized what his father had done: he had fulfilled his promise. By deliberately giving a wrong answer, he had ensured that Corax wouldn't be freed. And now Gabriel seized his opportunity.

He reached past the ring of blue flame and gripped his father's rune. It was cold, colder than ice. He lost all feeling as his fingers closed tightly around it.

"Wait, what are you doing?" asked Septimus.

"He told me to do the right thing," replied Gabriel. "So I'm doing it!"

"But that's not Corax's rune," protested Septimus.

"You want to free Corax? Do it yourself," Gabriel answered. "I'm rescuing my dad."

"You'll end up in another one," Septimus warned. "Just like them. How would it be, the three of you lined up like knickknacks on a mantelpiece until kingdom come? Oh, there must be a better way!"

As Septimus complained, Pamela leaned down and peered at Corax's stone. In the very center, the dark figure with enormous wings turned, as if aware of some sound, far away.

She peered closer. The figure moved slightly. Could he see her? Did he know she was his daughter? According to Aunt Jaz, he had no clue. Yet here, now, she felt his presence and it was growing upon her, like a creeping chill, advancing toward her heart.

Pamela shivered. Inches away, Gabriel was trying to rescue *his* father while she was staring at *her* father, with no desire to free him. *Is there something wrong with me,* she wondered, *that I don't feel what Gabriel feels?*

Pamela felt herself slowly pulled forward. It was gentle at first, but it became stronger, a power moving her toward the silhouette, drawing her fingers into the flames, toward the stone—it was so strong she almost couldn't resist. If her fingers were to touch the rune, she would be bound to answer a riddle. She would have to risk her freedom for the Lord of Air and Darkness.

Suddenly, however, strong hands gripped her and pulled her backward. "Careful!" Somes whispered.

Pamela sank to the ground, utterly drained. She saw Gabriel waiting for the words to form on the ceiling, his hands still tight around the rune.

"Hey, if I don't get it right?" said Gabriel. "You guys should all just go home."

He met their eyes, one by one.

When he looked back at the ceiling, the riddle was forming into familiar words.

What must be answered, but never asks a question?

Gabriel exhaled and repeated the riddle to himself. "Never asks a question . . ."

Behind him, Abby repeated the riddle to herself several times.

"A fire alarm!" shouted Gabriel.

"Wait, that doesn't sound right," gasped Abby. "Gabriel, oh, why didn't you wait for me? You don't exactly 'answer' a fire alarm. The right word is . . . a *doorbell*. A doorbell must be answered! They don't ask questions."

She was too late. There was another earsplitting roar and Gabriel disappeared.

The blue flames flickered and flared around the pedestal. Another rune appeared beside Adam's.

Abby, Somes, and Pamela stared with horror at the silhouette inside it, for they recognized their friend, turning to survey his new prison.

"Oh, Gabriel!" Pamela cried, a tear rolling down her cheek.

"It's a lesson for all of us to mind our own business," said Septimus. He clapped his hands soberly. "Terrible indeed. I don't think anyone should dare tamper with these. It's madness." He attempted a cheery smile. "If we hurry now, we'll get back in time for dinner."

"Are you nuts?" snapped Abby. "We can't leave Gabriel's whole family here."

"Are you proposing that we *all* get snared in this monstrous nightmare?" replied Septimus. "Because I'm not—"

"There's another problem," interrupted Somes. He touched his ear, drawing their attention to a sound. It was distant but distinct: the cry of birds, echoing somewhere beyond the chamber, in the massive underground cavern.

"Oh, terrific." Septimus gave a sarcastic laugh. "Valravens. They're coming because you little monsters scared away the subterranean rock boa. We'll never get out of here alive."

Mopping his forehead with a handkerchief, he let out a whimper. "Do you see how foolish it was to scare away the serpent? We're potted, planted, and pickled. They'll snack on us as if we were bacon-wrapped figs at a smorgasbord."

Abby glared at Septimus. "I'm not leaving without Gabriel."

"Very well," said Septimus. "I'm off. I'll tell your parents that you died bravely." He walked toward the doors, then turned his head to deliver one last remark. "It would take a century-old genius with a library of encyclopedias to answer these riddles, not some pigtailed brat."

Abby threw her hands into the blue flames and grasped Gabriel's stone.

"Abby!" cried Somes. "I don't want to lose you!"

A crushed smile appeared on Abby's face. "Oh, Somes, that's the nicest thing you've ever said."

She gazed back at him with sweet affection, but suddenly her body went rigid. Her eyes settled on the letters appearing on the ceiling.

When does a stopped clock tell the correct time?

Think, Abby, think, she said to herself. *Even a stopped clock is correct once every twelve hours. So the answer is . . .* "Twice a day!"

The newest rock tottered on the pedestal, then went *poof!*, collapsing into dust. Gabriel appeared on the floor before them, looking quite stunned. "Did I get my answer right?" he asked.

"Nope," said Somes. Then he grinned and helped Gabriel to his feet. "Luckily, Abby got you back."

"Abby . . . ," said Gabriel.

But Abby reached for Adam Finley's stone and raised her eyes to the ceiling.

The riddle was not so simple this time. As she read it, her lips moved, forming each word slowly.

What has rivers but no water,
Mountains but no rocks,

Valleys but no grass,
Islands but no sand, and
Countries, though not a soul in them.

"Rivers but no water, mountains but no rocks . . ." The fact that the riddle made no obvious sense seemed to please her. Her eyes widened slightly. "Interesting," she murmured. "Sounds like a thing that represents all these places. A sketch? A photograph? No, wait, I've got it, the answer is a *map!*"

Poof! The rock collapsed. Adam Finley materialized on the floor and slowly stood up.

"Whoa!" said Somes. "Way to go, Abby!"

The triumph of answering two correct riddles had made Abby bolder, and she immediately threw her fingers around the next rune.

In what country do tall bears sleep?

"Oh, I know this one!" said a voice behind them.

Somes turned around and saw Septimus. He had been so astonished by Abby's success that he had crept back from the doorway and was now quivering with excitement. "Really," he insisted. "I believe I actually know this answer."

"Quiet!" Adam snapped.

Abby bit her lip. "Well, it sounds like a pun. Probably a silly one. What's another word for a country?" She paused, then nodded. "Of course. Bears sleep in hibernation." Then she laughed. "Oh, it's a *really* stupid pun! A country where tall bears sleep is a *high bear nation!*"

The sound of the next rock shattering was like a crack of thunder. It echoed through the chamber, repeating over and over, for half a minute. Like an ancient jail door releasing its longest-held prisoner, the rune made a noise like grinding iron as it dissolved into rusty powder.

A woman appeared before them, cross-legged and serene. Her short blond hair was wrapped tidily in a faded bandanna, and she was dressed in worn denim overalls and a peasant shirt. She surveyed her surroundings with gentle curiosity, and eventually settled on the faces of the children.

"Tabitha?" said Adam, kneeling beside her.

His voice made her smile, but she was puzzled. "Where am I?"

"You're safe," said Adam. "We've got you back, my love."

"Adam?" She peered at him. "What's happened to you?"

Adam laughed. "Oh! I'm older, that's all. It's been twelve years. *Twelve long years.*"

He beckoned to Gabriel and placed a hand upon his shoulder. "This is Gabriel, your son."

Tabitha stared at Gabriel for a long, confused moment. The boy looked familiar because he resembled his father, but it was something else that convinced her of who he was. The earnest anticipation in his face was unmistakable—the look of a child waiting for his mother, waiting for a very long time.

"Hi," he said.

"Gabriel," she whispered.

As they embraced, everybody else gathered around—

except Septimus, who interrupted the warm reunion by clapping his hands like a bell captain. "Ladies and gentlemen! Please? If I could have your attention, could you move aside, as I need a word with this young lady?" He stepped toward Abby. "My dear, such an impressive performance! I really am in awe of your intellect."

"Not bad for a pigtailed brat, huh?" said Abby.

"A rash remark," admitted Septimus. "Forgive me. Now, may I ask a small favor?"

"No, I will not bring back Corax."

Septimus nodded respectfully. "Understood, my dear. But I miss my feathered friend here." He gestured toward the stone containing Crawfin. "Perhaps you could bring my good raven back?"

"Well, I suppose so," said Abby. She was feeling pretty confident now, and without thinking about the risk, she plunged her hands into the flames.

"Abby, no!" cried Somes.

"It'll just be a sec—" she said as her body went rigid.

This time, however, the words overhead formed the hardest puzzle she had ever seen. Gabriel came forward to read it:

"My home and I are bound as one.
Never do we part.
My home it roars and crashes, but
I'm quiet (for my part).

"Some say I am the faster one
(My home moves all the same).
And when I die you can be sure
My home will still remain.

"I live my life within this home
Its qualities I cherish,
If I left it for a day,
You can be sure I'd perish."

Abby stared at the puzzle for a long time without saying a word.

"Could it be a snail shell?" asked Somes.

"Well," said Abby, "a snail's shell is strong and lasts longer than the snail does. But it doesn't roar and crash—though an empty shell can sound like the sea. And the line about being the faster one confuses me, too. The only answer I can imagine is a hermit crab's shell, because a hermit crab can leave it, but not for very long. . . . So that's my answer. A hermit crab and its shell."

"Wait!" cried Gabriel.

An earsplitting roar shook the room.

Gabriel put a hand to his head. He realized the answer too late. "It's a fish, and its home is the sea, which roars and crashes."

"Abby!" cried Somes.

❧ Noble and True ❧

A new stone appeared behind the blue flames. Gabriel and Somes peered at the silhouette of a girl with pigtails (and a bare patch where one was missing).

"Abby?" Gabriel whispered, but she showed no sign of hearing him.

Pamela turned fiercely to Septimus. "You and your selfishness! You should have been the one to guess that riddle. You'd better get her back!"

"I'm—I'm hopeless at riddles," whimpered Septimus. "I can't tell a grackle's egg from a waffle tick."

"Well, we have to do it," said Gabriel. "I'm not leaving her here."

He was about to put his hand on the stone when Somes seized him roughly and shoved him backward. "Don't, Gabriel," he said. "It should be me."

"Wait," argued Gabriel. "*I've* got the best chance of guessing the riddle."

"But we're all in this together, right?" said Somes. "And you've already been inside one of those things." His glasses were fogging up, so he tore them from his face and rubbed them fiercely. "It's got to be me."

"You guys," urged Pamela, "Septimus should be the one to put his hand on the stone."

"P-p-put *my* hand on the stone?" Septimus backed away. "Oh, I couldn't. *I daren't.* What if I get stuck in a stone? I get hives in cramped places."

"Hives? *That's* what you're worried about?" said Somes. Exasperated, he lunged forward and threw his hands into the flames. As his body stiffened, he clenched his jaw.

Gabriel spoke to him with soothing assurance. "Chill, Somes, okay? Keep a clear head."

Pamela put a hand on Somes's shoulder. "Noble Somes," she added affectionately.

Somes grimly raised his eyes to the ceiling as letters formed.

My name means "friend,"
I'll come when you call.
Take a letter from me,
And one becomes all.

A word that means friend, thought Gabriel. *Pal? Buddy? Amigo? Amicus?*

"Comrade? Classmate?" said Pamela, trying to be helpful. "More than a friend, someone in hard times who will come when you call."

"Take a letter away, and one becomes all," murmured Somes. "Could the word have *all* in it? What word means 'friend,' and contains the word *all*?"

"Ball!" shouted Septimus. "Squall! Gallstone?"

"Oh, Septimus, you're no help," said Pamela.

"Times of trouble," whispered Somes. "Well, in a war, you have an *ally*. That's a friend. Oh! Wait a minute. If you take the 'y' from *ally*, you get *all*."

Gabriel grinned. "Excellent, Somes!"

Somes took a deep breath. He swallowed and looked at his friend's silhouette. *Abby*, he thought, *I'm sorry for every dumb thing I ever said to you. And I hope this works.* Then he peered up at the words on the ceiling and said, "The answer is *ally!*"

There was a *poof* and the stone collapsed in a pile of dust.

Abby appeared in front of the pedestal. She looked up anxiously. "Has it been a hundred years?"

"More like a hundred seconds!" Somes said, laughing, as he helped her up.

"Welcome back, my dear," said Septimus. "That was an unexpected mishap, eh? I'm sure you'd like to give it another try? Hmm? One last little riddle?"

Adam Finley blocked the pedestal.

"That's enough, Septimus," he said.

The faint shriek of valravens echoed from the chamber doorway and stirred everybody to get going.

Septimus kneeled hastily by the rune containing his raven, Crawfin. The old man's face became full of regret.

"I miss you, old friend," he whispered, his lips trembling. "But I'm a milksop, a feeble, custardy coward." Then he turned to the stone containing Corax's shifting silhouette, and his expression hardened into disgust. "Another time, Your Eminence."

When they were out of earshot of Septimus, Gabriel whispered to Mr. Finley, "Dad? Did you *really* mean to get that riddle wrong?"

"I certainly did," said Mr. Finley. "I wouldn't bring Corax back for anything."

"But that means you knew I would—"

"I knew you would do the right thing," said Mr. Finley. *"And* do it better than I could."

"But you risked . . ."

Mr. Finley smiled faintly and reached for Tabitha's hand, as if to remind Gabriel that it was all worth it.

They were a large group now. They shuffled as quickly as they could along the curved blue corridor, gathered the bundle of coats and headlamps, and emerged upon the rocky plateau with granite walls rising dramatically around them.

As they surveyed miles of vast, gloomy cavern, they could all see a cluster of yellow eyes in the distance. The birds were flying along the walls of the immense underground domain, and would reach them soon.

"No talking," whispered Adam. "If we get down into the

twisting passageways of the maze, they won't be able to follow."

Quickly, they descended into the maze and hurried down the first right-hand turn. The cries of the birds faded. Pamela and Somes were last, and once he felt safe, Somes stopped to tie the snapped lace of one of his sneakers. In that brief moment, the other members of the group proceeded to another fork and turned.

By the time Pamela and Somes got there, they couldn't see anyone. They called after the others, but the earthy walls and sharp turns muffled all sound.

"Which way do we go?" whispered Pamela. "Do you remember whether we were supposed to keep to the right wall or the left wall?"

"Hey, everybody!" cried Somes.

But no answer came.

Somes heaved a sigh. "I don't think anyone said. So let's go . . . left."

"Yes, that's what we did when we entered," agreed Pamela. "But shouldn't we stay to the right when we leave?"

"I don't know. Maybe it doesn't matter," said Somes. "I can't remember what Mr. Coffin said."

They decided to keep left, and followed the cramped dark passage as it twisted down dead ends, brought them back out, then turned and twisted again.

After about fifteen minutes, Somes and Pamela sensed a change. The air became warmer. They had arrived at a higher point in the cavern. They tied their jackets around their waists.

"I don't remember this at all," murmured Pamela.

"Me neither," said Somes, and then he squinted at something ahead. "What's that?"

It was a series of flickering torches, coming from what seemed like the very end of the maze. They looked cheery and welcoming. Somes and Pamela removed their headlamps and clambered from the tunnel up steps leading to a polished granite balcony carved out of the cavern wall; it was cream colored and veined with gold, and it revealed a spectacular view: the ruins of Aviopolis, stretching out for miles beneath them.

In the gray gloom, they spied a great tower lying upon its side in fragments. Columns of vast temples tipped against each other like fallen dominoes, and a series of stone bridges zigzagged this way and that, some with spans that rose high and stopped abruptly where they had crumbled or collapsed.

Statues dotted the ruins, some human, others an unlikely combination of bird and beast. Everywhere, the walls, pillars, and rubble glistened, flecked with quartz and alabaster.

"Hello?" said a voice. "Who's there?"

Pamela jumped with surprise. A boy was sitting at the farthest end of the balcony, swinging his bare feet. He had long, curly dark hair that swept over his shoulders, and he was wearing a threadbare pair of jeans and a T-shirt.

"I'm Pamela," she said. "That's Somes."

The boy smiled. "My name's Cassius. Where'd you come from?"

"From Brooklyn," replied Somes.

The boy sprang off the balcony. "Come see where I live," he said, and gestured for them to follow him into a chamber that appeared to have been scooped out of the cavern wall.

Inside, it was a grand-looking place, with pillars of pink granite and black amethyst and polished floors tiled in precious stones. It was also messy, like a playroom. Clothing was strewn over chairs of garnet, aventurine, and opal; open paperback books lay on every surface; and boxes of cereal, raisins, and crackers were scattered across tabletops. A water fountain bubbled out of the mouth of a carved fish into a marble basin. A bed with a headboard of polished jade was covered with a heap of sheets and cushions.

Cassius regarded Somes with fascination. "Wow, you're tall," he said. "How old are you?"

"Twelve."

Grinning, Cassius puffed out his chest. "Me too! Are you hungry, Somes?" He picked up a box of crackers and presented it to him.

Somes took the box, though he didn't really want to eat. He noticed that it had claw marks.

Cassius offered Pamela a small box of raisins. "You must be hungry, too," he said.

"Thank you," said Pamela. "How long have you lived here?"

"I don't know." The boy shrugged. "I've been here with my dad for as long as I can remember."

"Where's he?"

"He disappeared about a month ago, when the tower fell." Cassius pointed to the great structure that lay in fragments beyond the balcony. "I've looked for him all over, but . . ." The boy's expression changed slightly; then he picked up a jar of peanuts and nibbled a few.

"And you've been here all that time with nothing to do, all alone?" asked Pamela, her voice full of sympathy.

"Oh no," Cassius replied boldly. "I mean, I read and play, and I'm not alone. I have the birds to keep me company."

"*Birds?*" Somes replied sharply.

Cassius jumped up and whistled toward the ruins. Far away, a fierce *CAW!* echoed. Somes and Pamela stiffened with alarm.

"Don't be afraid," said Cassius. "They'll do anything for me. Silly birds."

In a few moments, a cluster of glowing yellow eyes approached and alighted on the balcony. Somes recognized the valravens everybody had spotted before—tatty-feathered creatures with jagged, whitened beaks.

Seeing the visitors, the phantoms hissed and glared, raising their neck feathers in anger.

"Behave yourselves!" the boy snapped. "These are my friends, Somes and Pamela. Be nice."

The valravens crouched at the boy's command, dropping their hackles. Cassius stroked them, and they made a meowing sound, like wailing kittens.

"See? They're my pets." He introduced the birds, one by one. "Bumper! Thumper! Skimpy! Dimpy . . . and the one with the mangled right claw is Lefty."

"Lefty?" Somes smiled in disbelief.

Pleased by Somes's reaction, Cassius got excited. "He does tricks," he said. "Want to see? Here—" He took the cracker box from Somes. "Lefty? Fetch! *Fetch!*" He spun a cracker into the air above the valraven.

The valraven uttered a squawk, and its head shot into the air—without its body—and captured the cracker in its beak. As the head dropped, the valraven's body hurriedly hopped into position so that its head landed exactly upon its neck.

Cassius turned to Somes with a grin. "How cool is that?"

"Epic," admitted Somes.

"I'll show you something else!" cried Cassius, leaping up and running into a room adjacent to the chamber.

Somes frowned and turned to Pamela. "So? You realize who he is, don't you?"

"Yes." Pamela sighed, surveying the messy chamber. "My poor brother. His whole life has been spent down here with no mom, a disappeared dad, and those birds. I feel so sorry for him."

"Your *valraven* brother," emphasized Somes. "What happened to his wings? Is he human by day and valraven by night?"

Pamela glared at Somes. "He's my *brother*."

"So?" Somes shrugged. "That's the only thing you know."

"I can see he really likes you, Somes," she whispered. "Did you notice how he tried to impress you?"

"Big deal," grumbled Somes.

"Well, I think Cassius is nice. He belongs with his family, not living in the darkness here, all by himself. He's just like us."

"Hey, look at this!" cried Cassius, coming out of the shadows. He was holding a long stick. "I found this in the ruins a few days ago. I think it's special. It has a tingly feeling. Here, touch it." He offered it to Somes.

The moment Somes grasped the stick, he felt an intense warmth emanate from the wood through his fingertips, and he guessed that it was the staff Gabriel had lost during his previous adventure in Aviopolis. Gabriel had explained to Somes that it was made from the wood of an ash tree, known in mythology as the Tree of Life, and it was magically linked to the torc. For example, he could summon the torc with the staff—it would come flying through the air and wrap itself around the ash-wood stem. The staff could also destroy valravens, bursting them into feathery explosions.

As he dusted the staff off, Somes wondered if it still held any power. He pointed it toward the valravens on the balcony. The startled phantoms took off in a flurry of panic.

"I should have warned you," said Cassius, laughing. "They hate that stick. I don't know exactly why."

"Gabriel will be so glad that you found this, Cassius," said Pamela.

"Who's Gabriel?" asked Cassius.

"Oh—" Pamela hesitated, wondering if this was the right time to explain.

"He's a really good friend," interjected Somes. "You should meet him."

Pamela shot a relieved glance at Somes, and he nodded back to her.

"You really should," said Pamela. "Want to come with us? We're going back to Brooklyn."

Cassius hesitated before answering. "Is it close by?" he said. "I knew the cavern was big, but I didn't know anybody else lived here."

"Well, it's not exactly *here*. It's up there," said Pamela, raising her eyes.

Cassius followed her glance, and for the first time, he looked afraid. "Up *where*?"

"Brooklyn is a place aboveground," said Somes.

"It's full of people, trees, houses, parks, grocery stores, blue skies, clouds—"

Cassius began twisting a strand of his hair as Pamela talked. "Oh, sure," he interrupted. "I've read about those things. I know what they are. But they're just in stories, aren't they?"

"Come and see. You can stay at my house," said Pamela.

"Or stay and wait for your dad," added Somes. "It's up to you."

Cassius drew a breath, then peered beyond the balcony to the fragments of the fallen tower. An expression of solemn resolve came over his face. "I'll come," he replied. "Hey, Somes? You can keep that stick, as a present. My birds hate it anyway."

"Thanks," said Somes, tightening his grip on the staff.

Pamela told Cassius to bring a change of clothes and a toothbrush, but Cassius said he was ready to go as he was. Somes suggested shoes, but Cassius explained that the soles of his feet were tough from years of running around barefoot.

Once they set off, Cassius started to look around for his valravens. At the mouth of the maze, he called them, and they landed in a row on his arm. He stroked their heads, one by one.

"Bumper? Thumper? Don't be mean to Skimpy. And you, Dimpy, take care of Lefty, okay?"

The birds protested with a chorus of meows. Cassius scratched their neck feathers and consoled them. "Don't cry. I'll be back soon," he said.

Reassured, the birds flew off into the cavern. Cassius turned away from Pamela and Somes to wipe tears off his cheeks, then followed the two friends into the maze.

❋ Corax's Second Chance ❋

Gabriel was near the entrance to the maze. At each turn, he felt his mother's hand upon his, squeezing tightly, just to remind him that she was there. He had so much to tell her— twelve years of his life to explain. He wondered where to begin.

When he and his mother took the last fork, and the passage ahead became straight and steep, Gabriel waited for the rest of the group to catch up. As Septimus walked past him, he noticed an odd design on the back of the man's coat. It was a ring, about the diameter of a dinner plate, like a burn mark.

Abby joined Gabriel. "Isn't that weird?" she whispered. "I wonder if he left it on a stove or something."

Gabriel turned back to the maze. "Hey, where are Somes and Pamela?"

"They can't be far," said Abby.

"When was the last time you saw them?"

Abby breathed on her glasses and rubbed them. "Now that I think about it—almost an hour ago."

They turned and walked back to the last fork in the passageway.

"Could they be lost?" wondered Abby.

At that moment, Gabriel felt something crunch beneath his feet. He kneeled down and noticed some bright red pistachio shells on the dirt floor. "Abby, look," he whispered.

"Pistachio nuts. So?"

"Red pistachios. Pleshette rewarded Punch with them at the shop. What if he's here with that monkey?"

"Why would they come here?" Abby replied.

"Paladin heard that Pleshette was upset about the duds and bribed Burbage to show him the way to the chamber. He wants those diamonds, and Punch is amazing at riddles."

Abby picked up her pace through the passage. "No kidding. If Corax is set free by the monkey, then Snitcher will give him the torc and—"

"It would be the end of everything," murmured Gabriel.

By this time they were running back into the maze. Gabriel hoped that his parents would continue forward with Septimus. Nothing mattered more than stopping Pleshette and the monkey. They followed the passage's twists and turns as fast as they could.

"Gabriel? What do we do when we get there?"

"Simple," said Gabriel. "We destroy Corax's rune. It's what I should've done before we left the chamber."

"How do you destroy a rune?" asked Abby.

"I saw it happen in Pleshette's shop," he explained. "When I was with Paladin in the cage, Pleshette tapped one with a hammer. The rune shattered, and the person trapped inside appeared. He was a dwarf holding a sword. He tried to attack Pleshette, but then he exploded."

"Cool," said Abby.

"Yeah, I think the penalty for taking a rune from the chamber without answering a riddle is to lose it forever."

"What a wicked way to go. Death by exploding." Abby frowned. "Though it is the perfect way to get rid of a really bad dude. I think it's a good plan, but suppose Pleshette is already there?"

Gabriel looked at Abby grimly but said nothing.

The two ran faster, hoping luck would be on their side. Gabriel dragged one finger against the wall, turning left, then right, then right again, then left.

"Let's hope that Burbage gets lost in here and never finds his way to the chamber," he said.

When they arrived at the curved passageway lined with lapis lazuli, they were hot and sweaty. Dropping their gear, they caught their breath, then tiptoed forward.

"Oh no," said Abby.

The great brass doors of the chamber were cracked open, and Pleshette stood in the domed room, staring at the pedestal. His shaved head matched the smooth dome of the ceiling. He had unbuttoned his raincoat. Burbage was perched upon his left shoulder and Snitcher nestled upon the right. There was no sign of Punch—but Gabriel felt more concerned about Snitcher.

"Remember, that robin can turn us into grubs if he wants to," he whispered.

At that moment, Pleshette uttered a triumphant chuckle. "Great heavens, look at them, Burbage! They're perfectly preserved! How could I have let Septimus fool me with those fakes? These are a marvel to see."

In the first rune, a raven preened its feathers. In the other, a silhouette of a half man, half valraven crouched, his wings beating.

Snitcher gave a triumphant chirp. "Great lord and master, how I've waited for this moment!"

The robin's voice changed tenor and became deep and booming. "Indeed, Snitcher, the end of my captivity is near. I ache to be back in my own body, to rule my subjects and make my enemies tremble!"

Pleshette stared at the robin. "Who just spoke?"

"I am Corax, Lord of Air and Darkness. My spirit resides in this robin, though my body is bound by magic in that wretched stone. Be quick and begin my release. My valraven army waits anxiously for my return. You'll get your payment soon enough."

The shopkeeper adjusted his eyeglass lenses to assess the robin's sincerity. "Prove it."

"You have my word. An army of valravens waits above-ground. After freeing me, you shall emerge from this cavernous domain and find yourself showered in diamonds."

Dazzled by this prospect, Pleshette decided to take the risk. "Very good, Your Eminence. How do we begin?" he said.

"Read the writing above you," barked the robin in a deep baritone. "And pay heed to its warning."

As before, the letters on the domed ceiling began to take recognizable form, and their message was the same sober warning that Adam Finley and Septimus had encountered—inviting every newcomer to reach for the rune and deliver the riddle's true answer, or fail and become a prisoner with the circle of fire.

When he had finished reading, Pleshette began searching his pockets. "Punch!" he cried. "Where are you?"

"Oh, what a creep," Abby whispered to Gabriel. "He's going to make the monkey do it."

The small capuchin monkey crept out of Pleshette's left raincoat pocket and quivered at the sight of the gray raven.

"Punch," said Burbage, "grab that stone with the raven inside . . . or I shall eat your tail!"

Curling his precious tail tightly around one leg, the monkey reached through the flames and toward the rune containing Crawfin. The moment Punch's fingers touched the stone, his body stiffened in terror. His eyes rose to Pleshette, who watched the Gutnish letters slowly transform into a riddle.

A pencil needs one,
A ballerina performs on one,
Every decimal has one.
What is it?

Punch frowned, then uttered a triumphant shriek. "Point, point, point!"

The rock collapsed into dust and a magnificent white raven materialized before them. He flapped his wings and looked around, as if stirring from a deep sleep. Recognizing the gray raven, he narrowed his eyes.

"Brother Burbage? Where am I?"

"You are in the Chamber of Runes, dear brother Crawfin," said the gray raven. "I've set you free."

"Did not!" Punch interjected. "I did!"

The white raven looked puzzled. "Where is Septimus?"

"He put you here," grunted Burbage. "Deserted you. If I hadn't come to free you, you'd still be encased in rock, like *that* one." The gray raven tipped his beak at the rune containing Corax.

"Truly? Septimus didn't try to free me—his own amicus?"

"Indeed."

The white raven gave a bitter shrug. "Humans are all the same. They use us, then betray us. They can't be trusted."

The two ravens took to the air and flew through the brass doors of the chamber so swiftly that they didn't notice Gabriel and Abby huddled in the doorway.

Snitcher hopped on Pleshette's shoulder. "Now it is time for my master's liberation."

Pleshette propped the monkey before the pedestal. "Again, Punch. Let us proceed."

"Don't, Punch!" shouted Gabriel, who had chosen this moment to step forward. "If you guess wrong, you'll be stuck in a rune, too."

"And Pleshette will leave you in it forever," added Abby.

Pleshette spun around and glared at them. "You again? Go away!" he snapped. "Little troublemakers. Haven't you cost me enough already?"

The monkey, however, seemed to be considering Abby's words. He searched Pleshette's face for a hint of compassion, but the shopkeeper's greedy eyes were fixed on the stone beyond the dancing blue flame.

"Get on with it," he said. "I'll soon be richer than Croesus!"

Regarding his master with dismay, Punch whispered to himself with disgust, "Don't be stupid, stupid, stupid."

Suddenly, Pleshette grabbed Punch and tried to thrust him through the flames. The monkey shrieked, tore at Pleshette's cheek with his hand, then leaped over him and scuttled down the passageway.

"We don't need him, Pleshette!" roared the robin in Corax's deep, booming voice. "The boy can answer the riddle, and if he fails, we'll use the girl."

Pleshette nursed the scratch on his cheek and beckoned to Gabriel. "Come here, boy."

Abby shouted, "No, Gabriel! Don't!"

Pleshette seized Gabriel's hands and tried to thrust them into the ring of fire.

"REACH INTO THE FLAMES!" shouted Corax. "Or Snitcher shall wish you into a rune of your own!"

It was a terrible choice. Gabriel struggled against Pleshette's grip.

"Gabriel," Abby said, meeting his eyes, "don't forget what happened to the dwarf's rune."

"Fine," said Gabriel. "I'll do it. Just get your hands off me." The shopkeeper relaxed his grip.

Gabriel remembered that a rune could be smashed to smithereens. But how? he wondered. How did Septimus extract the dwarf's rune from the ring of fire without answering a riddle? This was the puzzle.

He turned to the dancing flames. *If I reach in, I won't be able to move. So how can I shatter it?*

"Gabriel!" said Abby, her eyes bright with inspiration. "Remember the *coat*!"

The coat? thought Gabriel. *What is she talking about?*

Scrutinizing the pedestal, and the fire that lapped around its edge, Gabriel had a piercing thought. The blue flames made a perfect circle. Where had he seen it before?

Suddenly, it came to him. The coat. Of course! Septimus's coat had a burn mark on it that was the exact same shape and size as the ring of fire.

"Okay," he said to Pleshette. "I'm ready."

"Hurry up!" cried the shopkeeper.

The robin's little black eyes darted suspiciously from Gabriel to Abby.

Gabriel removed his sweatshirt and took a deep breath.

Abby nodded slowly. "I believe in you, Gabriel," she said.

Gabriel smiled, then turned to the flames, but instead of reaching in, he threw his sweatshirt over the pedestal. For a brief second, the flames vanished, and smoke wafted through the sweatshirt.

Now Gabriel grabbed the rune with the fabric and slid it from the pedestal. The blue flames immediately started up again, but the pedestal was bare.

He raised the smoky bundle high over his head.

"What are you—" began Pleshette. "Don't!"

"Hurry!" cried Abby.

With all his might, Gabriel threw the rune down on the stone floor.

A brilliant blue light illuminated the room. A deafening crash, like a thousand shattering windowpanes, filled Gabriel's ears. The last rune vanished.

As the light faded, Corax rose before the pedestal, his enormous black wings flexing above him. He smirked at the boy with malevolent triumph as the excited robin fluttered about him.

"The Lord of Air and Darkness has returned!" chirruped Snitcher.

"Pathetic child," muttered Corax. "You thought you could destroy me? I'm free, and you are helpless to do anything about it."

Gabriel felt Abby's hand squeeze his shoulder. She was trembling.

Corax held out his sharp-taloned forefinger. "Come, Snitcher, you have served me well."

The robin alighted upon Corax's claw.

"You know what to do," said the demon, his jaundiced eyes glittering at the exuberant bird.

"I wish you to have the torc, Eminence."

At that instant, the silver semicircle tipped with two raven heads released its hold on the robin and floated up to rest around Corax's neck. It looked larger now, and all the more formidable.

"Mine at last," he said. "Oh, what shall my first wish be? So much to do."

But then Corax's knees buckled slightly. He looked surprised, and gasped, then doubled over, clutching his belly. "What is happening?" he groaned.

When the demon's knees struck the floor, Gabriel was not surprised, for he remembered seeing the same thing happen to the dwarf in Pleshette's shop.

Corax's wings fell slack, his head sank between his shoulders, and as he struggled for breath, his yellow eyes flickered toward Gabriel. "You *knew* this would happen!"

Gabriel nodded.

Corax struggled to fly, but fell clumsily back to the floor. "You've won," he whispered.

"I'm sorry," said Gabriel, watching the demon struggle to breathe.

Wrapping both arms around his belly, the winged ghoul tried to sit upright, but his head looked unbearably heavy and his eyes had dimmed. Something awful seemed to be happening inside him, and yet he appeared more puzzled by Gabriel's reply. "Why are you sorry?"

"I wish you could have been my uncle . . . and Pamela's father . . . and part of my family instead of what you are," Gabriel said sadly. "I wish you could have been . . . human."

"Human," echoed the feeble voice. "Human."

It was his last word.

The explosion in the chamber was deafening. A million bright, shining pieces burst into the air and swiftly darkened to fluttering black cinders. The ring of fire swelled into a hot ball and burst. The pedestal collapsed to dust. The strange words shimmering upon the domed ceiling faded into darkness as a huge crack spread across it and crumbled into thousands of fragments that rained down on the floor. The open chamber revealed the dark cavern walls above it as the explosion rumbled and echoed, back and forth, in shock waves that boomed through a thousand unseen pathways and passages. There were no more words, no riddles, no runes, and there was no need to free anybody from this place. With Corax destroyed, so were the torc and the Chamber of Runes.

Pleshette staggered to his feet. His pale pink head was scratched from the monkey's attack and smeared with ash from the explosion. He dusted the cinders from his raincoat and pointed a trembling finger at Gabriel.

"You ruined me!" he shouted weakly. "I've lost every-thing—my animals, my monkey, my living."

"Oh, and don't forget—he saved the world," said Abby. "C'mon, Gabriel, let's go home."

Dusting powder and cinders from their shoulders, Gabriel and Abby descended from the plateau back into the maze. Their coats and headlamps were lost in the debris, but they knew that as long as they followed the wall, they would find a way out.

In time, they heard voices close by.

". . . I think we're almost there," said a boy.

"Somes, is that you?" called Abby.

"Hey, Abby!" answered Somes.

After two more turns, Gabriel saw headlamps, and three figures appeared: Pamela, Somes, and a strange boy standing between them.

"Gabriel, Abby, this is Cassius. He's been living here in Aviopolis his whole life," Pamela explained.

Even at first glance, the link between this strange, lost boy and Pamela was obvious. He had the same dark eyes, long, curly hair, and look of yearning. It was easy for Gabriel and Abby to guess the boy's connection.

"Cassius's father has been missing for over a month," explained Pamela. "What happened to you guys? Did you get lost, too?"

"Totally," said Gabriel, who decided it was the wrong time to explain what had happened to Corax. "Good to meet you, Cassius," he went on. "Are you coming with us?"

"Is that okay?" replied the boy.

"Of course it's okay," said Abby, and she reached forward and shook Cassius's hand with a very sturdy grip.

Cassius looked at Abby, with her mismatched shoes, multiple sweaters, and pigtails. "Is this how girls dress in Brooklyn?" he asked.

"Nobody in the world dresses like Abby," said Pamela, laughing.

Then Somes remembered the staff. He held it out to Gabriel.

"Hey!" said Gabriel, taking it. "Where in the world did you find this?"

"Cassius found it in the ruins and gave it to me."

"Way to go, Cassius," said Gabriel.

Cassius dipped his head modestly.

They were all quick to move on. In a few more turns, they discovered the passageway that ascended the steep cavern. The return journey seemed faster, which probably had something to do with their high spirits, and presently they arrived at the brick-lined corridor with the rungs leading upward.

Voices echoed from above. "I tell you, I can only climb slowly! This is exhausting. My legs are wobbly," cried someone who sounded like Septimus.

"We're almost there, Septimus," replied Adam, who was pushing the old fellow up the rungs from behind.

"Dad!"

"Ah, Gabriel," said Mr. Finley, peering down. "We were just trying to decide whether to go back and look for you. Pick it up, old fellow. We're all here now."

They scrambled up the rungs and crept into the waning light of dusk. The streetlamps were turning on all over Coney Island.

❄ The Homecoming ❄

When the Finleys and their friends emerged from the manhole, Paladin and Vyka were waiting for them. The road was littered with bone fragments, beaks, claws, and heaps of black feathers. Paladin was quick to explain that the group had missed an immense battle between the valravens and the owls, which the owls had obviously won. All the bones wriggled, like pieces of some immense jigsaw puzzle attempting to reassemble itself.

"It'll probably take them years to get back together," sneered Septimus.

On the way to the subway station, they passed a group of reporters and photographers clustered around squad cars with lights flashing. The police and several detectives held up a plastic bag containing a dazzling array of diamond jewelry.

The white-haired commissioner stepped forward to speak: "I'm happy to report that the stolen diamonds are recovered!"

"Who recovered them?" replied a reporter. "Your crack team of detectives?"

"Er, no . . . it was owls," replied the commissioner.

The reporters all laughed as the bristling detectives stalked back to their cars.

On the subway ride home, Adam and Tabitha sat together, arms around each other, deep in conversation. Gabriel and Pamela had their ravens perched on their shoulders while they spoke with Abby, Somes, and Cassius.

"Okay," said Somes. "One thing has been bugging me about this visit to Aviopolis."

"What's that?" replied Gabriel.

"I'm very suspicious of Mr. Coffin. How did he know to give me a hook to open a manhole cover? And why did he tell us how to navigate a maze? I think he was up to no good."

"Somes," said Gabriel, smiling, "he's my aunt's boyfriend. Whatever he was up to, I think he's on our side."

"I'm not so sure," murmured Somes. "He's given me the worst grades of all my teachers. Maybe he was just trying to steer us to our doom."

"But he didn't, Somes," argued Abby. "It all worked out in the end, so I think your theory is ridiculous."

"Look," said Gabriel, "I'm sure Aunt Jaz knows the truth about him."

His friends laughed, because they were all aware that if Aunt Jaz (or anyone else in the Finley house) did know the truth, it might be a secret for many years.

The group parted ways on Fifth Street. Abby and Somes hugged the others and headed back to their homes. Septimus went grumbling down the hill, annoyed at having nothing to show for his dangerous journey. Pamela led Cassius and Tabitha Finley up the block toward the Finley house, while Adam lingered for a moment beside Gabriel.

"One thing, Gabriel," he said. "What was that terrible explosion? I thought I might have lost you forever. You can't imagine how relieved I was when you appeared at the end of the tunnel."

Gabriel explained that he and Abby had spotted the pistachio shells and found Pleshette in the chamber. "Anyway, I managed to destroy the last rune."

"And Corax? The torc? The chamber?"

"It's all over, Dad," said Gabriel with a weary smile.

Adam gave a sober nod. "Well done," he said. "Well done indeed."

Trudy was in an agitated state when the family arrived home. "Oh, Pamela! Adam! Gabriel!" she sputtered. "Where have you been? And who are all these people?"

Adam knew he had some difficult explaining to do. "Trudy! At long last, Tabitha is back from Iceland . . . ," he began. "She lost her passport twelve years ago. You wouldn't believe how complicated it was to get a new one. But here she is, and she brought her nephew!"

"Twelve years to get a new passport?" said Trudy. "That's the most ridiculous thing I have ever heard."

"And that is exactly what I told the man at the passport bureau," said Adam. Then he turned to Cassius and put his hands on the boy's shoulders. "I would like you to meet my nephew. This is Cassius."

"Cassius?" Trudy repeated. The moment she set eyes on him, she recognized his resemblance to Pamela—his long, curly dark hair, his brown eyes, and something else, lost in some foggy, forgotten region of her memory. She put her hand to her heart and stared at him with tender astonishment.

"Have we met before somewhere?" she asked the boy.

Cassius felt it, too. He smiled back at her. "A long time ago, maybe?"

"Oh, my goodness," she whispered. Trudy's cool stare became glossy with emotion; she uttered a gasp and suddenly hugged the boy very tightly. "What a special, special day!"

There was so much that needed to be explained to Cassius, but it could wait. The boy had found himself in a welcoming family, and after so many years of dark solitude, he was drenched in love, light, and more companionship than he had ever had before.

Although their school days now settled into a calmer routine, Gabriel and his friends often sat on his stoop and looked back over the adventure of the past month, pondering some of the mysteries they had never quite solved.

Abby, for example, brought up something that bothered her. "Gabriel?" she said. "Don't you think it's strange that the valravens never attacked your house before? It would have been so easy. The robin could have commanded them to do it a month ago."

"I think I know the reason," said Somes. "The robin used to peek in Gabriel's windows, so he must have seen Trudy, which means Corax saw her, too. He probably wanted to protect her."

"So you think Corax still loved her?" said Abby.

"Definitely," said Gabriel. "I think that was the only human part of him left—the part that loved Trudy."

They were curious about Pleshette, and took a detour on the way home from school one afternoon, expecting to find his shop boarded up or sold. Instead, they saw his shaved head glowing beneath a single lightbulb; he was doing crosswords at the counter and sipping tea from the magic samovar. There were no cages to be seen, and the monkey's urn was gone. They guessed that Punch never dared return after Pleshette tried to force him into the ring of fire.

As for Cassius, Mr. Finley had to fill out a stack of papers to get him enrolled in school. On the first day of class, Gabriel led his new cousin along a hallway crowded with students, and everybody seemed to notice something different about him. Students spun around, feeling his presence. Teachers forgot what they were saying when he entered the room. Maybe it was just his deep gaze, or perhaps there was a little bit of something else that made him different from any other human.

Late in the evenings, if they didn't have homework, Pamela and Gabriel would call to their ravens and paravolate. They flew a grand loop around the city, just to make sure all was well, swooping over Coney Island, past the glittering lights of the big rides and Tillie's lunatic grin.

They circled the hilltop cemetery, anxious to see if any yellow-eyed phantoms were lurking, but all they saw was a robin, pacing back and forth, back and forth, upon a statue of an angel.

And when they were all tired out, they flew back to the Finley house, where the stove always prepared hot chocolate for them. Tabitha Finley would hear it making its bonking noises and pad downstairs to listen to the children describe their adventures. She believed in talking birds, merging with ravens, and magic of every kind—after all, she had survived twelve years in the Chamber of Runes. Then, after everyone trudged to bed and all the lights were out, the Finley house appeared to be at peace.

Except for this.

Occasionally, on those moonless nights when the sky was especially dark and not a soul was on the street, a solitary black bird sprang from the window of that brownstone on Fifth Street and soared above the rooftops of Brooklyn. Not even the great horned owls went near this creature, for it was larger than any raven or owl and its bright yellow eyes glowed in the dark—just like a valraven's.

About the Author

George Hagen is the author of *Gabriel Finley and the Raven's Riddle*, which *School Library Journal*, in a starred review, declared, "A great read for fantasy lovers who have worn out their copies of Harry Potter."

He also wrote two novels for adults: *The Laments*, a *Washington Post* bestseller and recipient of the William Saroyan International Prize for Writing, which *Publishers Weekly* called "a funny, touching novel about the meaning of family," and *Tom Bedlam*, which was described by *Booklist* as "Dickensian in scope and spirit. . . . Shot through with humor, and populated with a cast of eccentric charmers."

George lived on three continents by the time he was twelve. The father of three children, he now lives in Brooklyn. To learn more, visit gabrielfinley.com.